Coombesford Calendar volume II

Happy reading!

Elizabeth Ducie

Elizabeth

A Chudleigh Phoenix Publications Book

Cover design: Getcovers, Ukraine

Internal illustrations: Otis Lea-Weston

ISBN: 978-1-913020-15-6

Chudleigh Phoenix Publications

For Michael

The Village of Coombesford

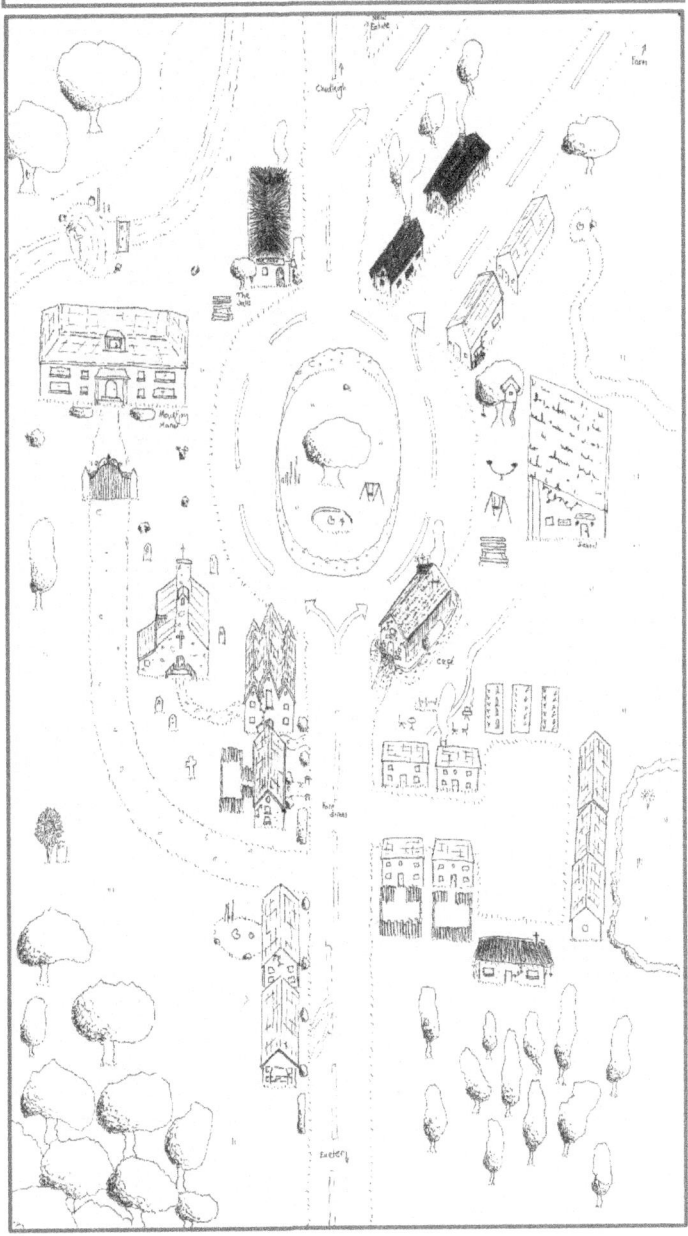

Contents

April: Josie's Front Door

"Josie's painting her front door green."

Annie's words rip through the hubbub of chatter in Cosy Corner as I sip my morning coffee.

"What did you say, Annie?" I'm certain I've misheard.

"Josie, her at No. 4. She's painting her front door green."

Annie, Betsy, and I have been friends for ever. Our little cluster of houses just off Fore Street has been the site of winter dinner-parties and summer garden-parties for as long as anyone can remember. We win 'Best Kept Street' most years.

Leaving my coffee unfinished, I hurry around the corner. Josie's our new neighbour; much younger than the rest of us, but it's good to have new blood; stops us getting set in our ways. At least, that's what I'd thought until now. Front doors aren't green; they're white. White doors, white window frames and black railings—that's what we've all got in Harcombe Close—until now. A green door—I ask you! She'll be putting up wooden shutters next and then, where will we be?

I know a full-frontal approach to the problem won't work. After all, she's bought the house; she has the right to do what she likes. Even so—a green door!

Next morning, I see Josie as she comes out of the Village Store. She's smiling to herself and humming a tune.

"Someone looks happy with life."

"Hi Eve; how are you? I've got to tell someone. I've met this guy, Patrick. He's the one who painted my door. He's over from Cork for the summer. We went dancing last night in Exeter and he's picking me up again in a while so we can go for a drive. Must dash—see you."

In a flash of patterned silk, she's gone, leaving behind a faint smell of lily of the valley. There's no chance to mention that door.

I don't see much of Josie for the next few days. There's a red sports car parked outside her door much of the time. Occasionally she and Patrick wander around the village, hand in hand.

Standing at the grocery counter in Cosy Corner one morning, I smell lily of the valley again. Josie heads straight for me with outstretched arm.

"Eve, do look; see what Patrick gave me last night!" She's wearing a thin gold bangle studded with emeralds. Tilting her head to the light, she shows off the matching studs in her ears.

"Eve, I know it's only been a short time—but I really think he's going to propose. Do you think I'd be rash to say yes? Should I ask for time to make up my mind? I really don't need it. I've known from the first moment I saw him. I'm so happy, I could dance!" She gives a couple of twirls and disappears out of the door and across the green. I still haven't solved the door problem.

I bump into Josie in Chudleigh library the following Saturday. She isn't wearing make-up or scent. She's frowning and doesn't see me at first.

"Oh, hello Eve. Sorry, I didn't notice you. Patrick? No I'm not seeing him today. He's got a friend over from Ireland. Apparently she just turned up on his doorstep and he feels he must look after her. Anyway, it gives me time to catch up on things. I know it's silly to feel jealous… he's just being kind, but…" As she turns away I see a glint of tears in her green eyes. I don't have the heart to mention the door.

For the next few days, Josie doesn't appear. There's no red sports car either. Finally, I walk across the road and knock on the green door. Still wearing her pyjamas, hair unbrushed and unwashed, Josie doesn't smell of lily of the valley today.

"Hello Eve, what do you want?"

"No one's seen you this week," I say, ignoring her manner, "and we're worried about you. Is everything OK?" She takes a deep breath and lets out a long sigh.

"Sorry—didn't mean to be rude. Come in. I'm just making coffee. Patrick?" She shakes her head. "His friend went back to Ireland, and he went with her. So that's it."

She moves around her little kitchen, fixing a tray and waiting for the kettle to boil. With her back to me, she carries on.

"To be honest, Eve, I'm relieved. It was all getting too intense."

So if she feels like that, why the unkempt look and reclusive behaviour?

"So Josie, if that's how —" She swings round, cutting across my question, as words tumble from her lips.

"The thing is, Eve, I feel such a fool. I'm sure everyone's laughing at me."

"Well, that's just nonsense," I say. "No-one's laughing at you. We're not like that in Coombesford." I finish my drink and put the empty cup on the draining board. Then I turn to her with my hands on my hips. "Now, I'm going to leave you to get washed and dressed. I'll be in Cosy Corner with the girls this afternoon. Come and join us—it's about time you got to know the others better."

She stands at the gate, watching me crossing the road. As I reach my gate, I turn back to her.

"And get that door changed right away. It'll remind you of him every time you see it—and green is such an unlucky colour."

We're sitting at our usual table just before three when Josie comes in. She's wearing a cotton frock printed with large flowers and a floppy straw hat. She's got her bounce back and smells of citrus. There's a streak of colour on her cheek that doesn't look like blusher. As she flops into a chair, she turns to me with a smile.

"Eve, I thought about what you said. I changed it straight away—and I did it myself this time. I found a beautiful shade of orange in the DIY store in Chudleigh."

Orange….orange! I splutter into my coffee. Suddenly, green doesn't seem so bad after all!

May: Cruising By Numbers

"Oh dear, someone's in for a damp few days," says the elegantly-dressed woman in the queue in front of me.

I hear her comment immediately after the splash.

"And such a distinctive bag too," her younger-looking male companion replies. The pair laugh and carry on up the gangplank.

I spin and grab the handrail, knowing what I will see, while praying I am mistaken. Floating in the grubby waters of the Hudson River is a suitcase; pale pink, with whorls of mint green and splashes of sunset orange. My suitcase!

As I watch my wardrobe for the next week gently bobbing just off stern, I think back to Mrs Christopher's whispered comment at the end-of-term assembly in July.

"The whole class contributed to the collection and Billy and Michelle came with me to make the choice." As the cheers of the children of Coombesford Primary School rang out, I'd beamed at the smiling faces of my reception class. In that environment, with friends and colleagues I'd known for twenty seven years, the suitcase seemed so appropriate; a wonderful accompaniment to my 'big adventure'. We'd planned the journey together over the past term; it had formed the basis of so many lessons: geography, obviously, but also maths, reading and writing. Now, floating in the rank river, the colours are too bright, out of place, just plain wrong. More 1960s than 1980s.

Two hours and an apologetic conversation with the Purser later, I follow a trickle of early diners down the staircase to the main restaurant. As it's the first night out, this will be an informal meal, which was just as well, seeing as my only dry clothes are the ones I was wearing when I boarded.

"This way, Ms Roberts," the *maitre d'* says, consulting his clipboard, "I believe you asked to be put on a table for eight."

"That's right," I reply, "I thought it was a good way to get to know people, learn the ropes as it were. It's my first cruise, you see, and I'm travelling alone." But even as he pushes my chair in under me and shakes my napkin across my lap, he's already fixing his eyes on the next couple waiting in line. I doubt if he even hears my words, let alone registers what I said.

"Well, enjoy your evening," he says—and is gone in a flash of polished shoe.

I'm the first to arrive at the table and spend the next few minutes happily people-watching. There are the old hands who know what to do and where to go, almost without being told. They look like they own the ship, rather than being mere passengers like the rest of us. There are others who are more hesitant, probably newcomers like me. Most of the passengers are elderly, around my age, I remind myself with a jolt, although there is a sprinkling of youngsters, many with Eastern European accents. Two things in particular strike me: everyone is part of a couple or a group; and no-one is stopping at my table.

"Are you ready to order, Ms Roberts," the waiter asks, holding his pencil poised over his pad.

"No, I'll wait until the rest of the table arrives," I smile at him. But the look on his face is enough to confirm what

I've already begun to suspect. "There isn't anyone else coming, is there?"

"No, Ms Roberts," he replies.

"But I asked to be put on a table for eight..." I suddenly realise the flaw in my plan. I've procured seven additional seats at my table; but I am not guaranteed companions to sit in them.

"Well, in that case," I sigh, "I'd better order—and please bring me the wine list!"

The lobster bisque is delicious and the cheese bread melts in my mouth. The glass of Californian Sauvignon Blanc is crisp and dry, with a 'hint of apples and new mown grass' just as the wine list promises. But what's the point of wonderful food if there's no-one to share it with? I can almost hear the comments at the other tables:

"She's obviously some-one who likes her own company."

"Maybe her companions are sea-sick."

"What — all seven of them?"

Nerves fading and appetite rapidly disappearing, I down the rest of my wine in one long gulp, then push back my chair and walk out.

The next day starts well. With my early morning tea, my steward brings the news that my clothes are being laundered and will be returned later. I decide to give the large dining room a miss and find a small tea room where I breakfast on coffee and Danish pastries. Not my usual muesli and fresh fruit, but if you can't break the routine when you're on holiday, when can you?

I stroll on deck in the early autumn sunshine, stopping to check the programme of lectures posted on the Purser's door, before returning to my cabin to find my clothes wearable once more—or at least some of them. I doubt if my crushed silk blouse will ever be the same again and I wonder if they even read the instruction label. My favourite evening cardigan is more off-white than apple-white. I am certainly going to need that claim form the Purser had offered me on the first evening—was that really less than twenty-four hours ago?

But at least, I now have clean underwear and an evening skirt I can wear to dinner. Things are starting to look up.

"Good evening, Ms Roberts." smiles the *maitre d'* as I enter the dining room that evening, "How are you enjoying your first cruise?" So maybe he was listening last night after all.

"Well, it's getting better," I say, "but I'm looking forward to having someone to talk to this evening. You haven't put me on another empty table, have you?"

"Of course not. In fact, your companions are already seated."

He points me across the dining room to a small oblong table in the corner. Three women are already seated, deep in conversation. One is middle-aged, with hair pulled back into a tight bun and a string of pearls straining to fit around the rolls of fat on her full neck. The other two look to be younger versions of their mother, which doesn't bode well for their futures. I smile at them as I pull out my chair.

"I believe this is my seat." There is a pause.

"Well, we specifically asked for a table for three," says the older woman with a sniff, "but I suppose it will be alright for you to sit there."

I grit my teeth and arrange my napkin on my lap, running through my list of stock topics for a suitable one with which to strike up a conversation. But it is too late. The three women have started chattering again—in French!

At least this time I make it to the end of the meal. As soon as their coffee is finished, my three companions—and I use that phrase lightly—throw their napkins on the table and leave, still talking intently. The youngest daughter gives me a timid smile as she passes, but her sister and mother seem to have forgotten my existence. So much for a pleasant evening's conversation. I sigh and drain my own coffee cup. As I stand up, there is a discreet cough at my elbow.

"Ms Roberts, you left without signing for your wine last night. I'm sure that was just an oversight, but if you could just..." the waiter proffers a leather folder with the cruise line's famous logo on one corner.

"I don't think so," I say.

He blinks.

"Excuse me?"

"I said, I don't think so." My voice sounds louder than usual and a little squeaky. People at the surrounding tables stop their conversations and look our way, but I am past caring.

"But, Ms Roberts, was there anything wrong with the wine? You didn't say."

"No, there was absolutely nothing wrong with the wine. In fact, that was one of the few things this company's managed to get right so far."

He stares at me open-mouthed as I start ticking off on my fingers:

"My bag ended up in the river; your laundry ruined my best blouse; last night you sat me at an empty table in the middle of a dining room of strangers; tonight you sat me with the French equivalent of Macbeth's three witches. I think the least you can do is give me a free glass of wine."

"But Ms Roberts..."

"And," I say, grabbing my handbag and pushing it under my arm, "I am a sixty-five year old spinster from England. Stop calling me Ms Roberts. Where I come from, people call me MISS," and turning on my heel, I march out of the dining room. I think I hear a smatter of applause behind me, but I don't pause to check. I head up the nearest staircase and out onto the deck. The clouds that masked the sun for most of the afternoon have all blown away and the stars are shining down from a sky of blue velvet. The moon is just a day off being full and standing in the stern, I stare at the silver pathway it makes across the churning water behind us. I take in a deep breath and let it out—very slowly.

When I return to my cabin, there is a half bottle of

champagne sitting open on the dressing table. I phone the Purser to say there's been a mistake.

"No Miss Roberts," says the quiet American voice at the other end of the phone, "there's no mistake. We realise we've not made a very good impression on you so far. This is our way of saying sorry."

"Well, you've got it wrong again, haven't you," I say. "If you think I paid for this cruise just to sit in my room and drink champagne on my own, you're sadly mistaken." I manage to keep calm while I replace the receiver gently on the cradle. Picking up the bottle, I walk to the sink and pour away a stream of fizzing, golden bubbles. Then, throwing myself on my bunk, like one of the children in my class, I cry myself to sleep.

"Someone looks deep in thought." I'm sitting in the sunshine finishing my breakfast tea the next morning, when the Purser pauses by my chair. I'm feeling more like my old self and just a little bit ashamed of my outbursts. I gesture for him to join me.

"I was just thinking about my reception class—well, Mrs Christopher's now, I suppose. It's the start of the new school year and there will be some nervous children arriving this morning. They'll soon make friends and sort themselves into groups, but I know how difficult it will be to start with."

"I'm sorry about the champagne; it was insensitive," he says. To my horror, I feel the tears well up again and blink rapidly, shaking my head. "We've made a real mess of things so far, haven't we?" he goes on. "What can we do to put it right?"

"Every term," I say, "I used to make a big thing about the first lunch; move the children around; make sure everyone had someone they could talk to. That way, there was no-one left on his or her own." He stares at me in silence then suddenly grins.

"Miss Roberts, I've got an idea," he says. "Will you give us one last chance to get it right?"

"Well, I'm not going anywhere, am I, young man?" I point out.

"OK, I'll come and collect you for dinner just before nineteen hundred hours this evening," and with a wave of his hand, he is off down the deck, leaving me to wonder what he has in mind. Although, so long as he manages to find me some real live passengers to talk to, frankly, I didn't care.

I decide to make a bit more of an effort in dressing for dinner this evening. As we were saying goodbye in New York, my brother thrust a parcel into my hands.

"Not quite your usual style, old girl," he said, "but we saw this in Jamaica and thought it would suit your colouring." 'This' turned out to be an ankle length cotton shift in iridescent greens and yellows. I'd pushed the parcel into my handbag, and so it had escaped the Hudson River and subsequent 'renovation' by the ship's laundry staff. I was uncertain when I first saw it, but had to admit it looked elegant and it is certainly cool.

At 6:59pm, there is a tap on my cabin door. Any doubts I'd had about the dress disappear at his reaction when I step out into the corridor.

"Wow, Miss Roberts, you look wonderful. Now, allow me to escort you to dinner."

When we reach the dining room, he sweeps straight past the *maitre d'* and leads me across the room to a table for eight. All the chairs are already full, apart from one, which he pulls out for me.

My neighbour is a woman in her forties with the sun-tan of someone who spends a lot of time in the open air.

"Miss Roberts, allow me to introduce my wife, Maisie," he says. "You two should have a lot in common. She hates this ship too!" and with a little bow, he is gone. I look at Maisie, feeling my face grow warm with embarrassment.

"Well, I'm not sure I'd use a word like 'hate'" I say.

"Oh, I would," she says with a grin. "When you spend

as much time at sea as we do, the so-called luxury quickly palls."

"So why do you do it?" The words are out of my mouth before I can stop them.

"Well, y'see, Phil and I have only been married a few years. His first marriage broke up because his wife couldn't take all the time at home on her own—found herself other entertainment, if you get my meaning."

I nod, unable to think of a suitable reply to this sharing of confidences so early in our acquaintance.

"So, when we got together, I was determined that wasn't going to happen. I gave up my job and I now join him on most of the crossings. Believe me, the novelty soon wears off."

I gaze at this woman with admiration. To give up everything to protect her marriage, what dedication!

"So how do you fill your time?" I ask.

"Well, to start with, I went to every lecture going, but there's only so much Greco-Roman architecture and medieval history one can take."

"Yes, I can see that."

"But now I've discovered something that's keeping me occupied for hours at a time. I've not managed to finish one yet—but I will; one of these days, I will." I stare at her perplexed, but suddenly the penny drops as I remember the press furore over a new craze recently arrived from Japan.

"You're talking about Sudoku, aren't you?" I ask.

"Yes! Have you discovered it too?"

"I certainly have; in fact, I've got a book of puzzles in my cabin."

"And can you do them?"

"Well, yes, most of the time—although some of the extra hard ones have defeated me."

"Miss Roberts, will you show me how to do them?" she pleads.

"Of course I will, Maisie—and my name's Carol, by the way." It feels so good, finally saying those words.

"What's that, Sudoku?" says a young man across the table. "Hey, I'd love to learn how to do those things; can I sit in on your lesson?"

"And do you have any idea how to finish a Kakuro grid?" someone else chips in. And suddenly, everyone at the table is nodding their heads and clamouring for help with the little maths puzzles that are rapidly taking the place of crosswords in the newspapers and the national psyche. By the time dinner is over, not only do I have seven new friends, but our first lesson is booked for the following day.

Maisie calls for me at nine thirty the next morning, grinning in anticipation. It appears that being the Purser's wife has some advantages and she'd been able to secure a flip-chart and pens.

"Although I've not managed to find an empty room that will accommodate all of us," she says. And that's how I come to be back in teacher mode, writing on the board in front of a group of eager students, in the lobby outside the main ballroom, on day four of the Atlantic crossing. It is all so familiar: the looks of puzzlement and concentration; the gradual smiles as understanding arrives; and the whoop of delight from Maisie when she finally achieves her first-ever Sudoku success.

"Miss Roberts, it's been a pleasure" says Phil the Purser as he stands at the top of the gangplank when we disembark in Southampton. "Maisie's absolutely buzzing with it—says she's ready to move on to Kakuro next time we sail."

"She's been a great student—and good fun to be with. Thank you for introducing us."

"We're always looking for new topics for lectures. How do you fancy coming back and repeating your success later in the year?"

I look around at the huge ship, remembering the first couple of days: wet clothes, and silent meals. But then I think of the friends I've made in the past few days, and smile at him.

"Young man," I said, "I wouldn't have missed this experience for the world. Where do I sign up?"

June: Playing The Field

Walking down Queen Street, she imagines she feels every eye burning into her back. The moon seems brighter than ever—and there are so many cars, so many people. Suddenly, she hears the last voice she wants to.

"Angela, what a nice surprise!" Her dad steps out of the paper shop, a handful of coins in his hand and a look of concentration on his face. Never good at maths, he's still suspicious of being short-changed by shopkeepers, more than a year after decimalisation has been completed.

"Hi dad, I thought I'd...," her voice fades away as the lie forming in her head refuses to reach her mouth.

"Good job I came out when I did," he said, "we'd have missed each other else—and you don't want to end up down that end of the street on your own at this time of night."

"Actually, Dad, I wasn't coming to meet you." She takes a deep breath and holds her head up high. "I was heading down there—there's something I need to do."

"At this time of night—there's nothing open apart from the chemist and that noisy new coffee bar." He stops suddenly and she holds her breath, waiting for the next sentence, watching the light dawn in his eyes. "Oh, I'm sorry, love. You were going to buy me some of that aftershave for my birthday, weren't you? I noticed they've got a special offer in the chemist's window. And now I've gone and spoiled the surprise." Taking her arm, he steers her back up the street towards the little two-up, two-down they've lived in since she was born. "Never mind, love, my birthday's not for another week—I'm sure you'll be able to think of another present by then."

Angela sits unseeing on the sofa all evening, ignoring her mum's attempts to involve her in discussions about the latest Coronation Street plot twists and not even pretending to be interested in Panorama, even though it's her dad's favourite programme, and she normally enjoys the chance to be deliberately provocative and challenge his traditional views. She's desperately trying to think of a reason, an excuse for not turning up at the coffee bar that evening. Anything to make Ahmed still love her, still want her to be his girl.

She's still tossing the question around in her mind when she arrives at the bus stop the next morning. She sees him before he sees her. He's lounging against the rail, chatting to some of his mates. When he turns and sees her, he stops talking and his dark eyes flash, as he strolls towards her.

"I waited for you last night. Where were you?"

"I'm sorry, I couldn't get away." She fails to think of a suitable excuse and opts for no explanation at all. Ahmed is not impressed.

"Well, you made me look a real fool, sitting there on my own," he says, "and nobody makes a fool out of Ahmed." Turning on his heel, he leaves her standing at the back of the queue while he saunters to the front and rejoins his mates. When the bus comes, the boys race to the upper deck. By the time Angela reaches the top of the stairs, they've taken all the seats at the back. Ahmed is hunched in an inside seat with one of his mates next to him. She tries to catch his eye, but he stares out of the window and ignores her. With a sinking heart, she takes a seat at the front and makes the journey alone, listening to the hoots of laughter coming from behind her. She knows they probably aren't talking about her, but she's not completely certain.

It's Tuesday and the whole morning is taken up with science and maths lessons. At lunchtime, there's a rehearsal for the school play, in which Angela has a minor role. She doesn't see Ahmed until mid-afternoon when they have an English Literature session together.

"Why are we reading this crap?" someone asks Miss Redwood, the young, newly-qualified teacher who only joined the school at the start of term. She blushes bright red, then throws the question back to the class.

"That's a good point, although I might not have phrased it quite like that. Any thoughts on why we're still reading Little Dorrit more than 100 years after it was published?"

As Angela's hand shoots into the air, she's aware of another arm waving from the opposite side of the room. Miss Redwood smiles at her encouragingly.

"Dickens' prose is timeless and speaks to us even today." Angela tries to ignore the low chorus of groans and jeers from her classmates as Miss Redwood nods then turns towards the other waving hand.

"Yes, Ahmed?"

"Much of the political commentary is as relevant today as it was in the 1850s."

Angela looks across at Ahmed and as their eyes meet, he smiles at her. It's like a cloud lifting from Angela's shoulders; suddenly everything seems just a bit rosier than it had before.

At the end of school, Ahmed is waiting for Angela when she walks down the steps. He takes her hand in his and the pair walk in silence across the school yard and down the road towards the bus stop.

"There's a disco at my sister's school this weekend," he says. "You will come with me, won't you?"

Angela just nods. She's so happy, she doesn't even start

to think about how she'll get permission to go.

It's not that Angela's parents are particularly old-fashioned or overly strict, although they are a good bit older than most of her friends' parents. "A late blessing on our marriage" is how her mum always explains away the fact that they are sometimes mistaken for her grandparents, rather than her parents. They just tend to be over-protective, especially where boys are concerned.

"Plenty of time for all that nonsense when you've finished all your exams," her dad is prone to say whenever Angela broaches the subject of boys, or going out, or taking time out of her studies. And most of the time, Angela's quite okay with this. In fact, she's secretly happy she hasn't got trendy parents like some of her girlfriends. Sophie's mum even offered to take her to the doctor and get her put on the pill as soon as she was 16—and then suggested they double-date. "That is so gross," was the general consensus on that type of parenting, even if Sophie's dad is long gone and her mum looks more like her slightly older sister.

At least, Angela used to be quite happy about this, but that was before she met Ahmed; before the handsome new boy arrived in class at the beginning of term and made a beeline for where she was sitting at the back of the class reading War and Peace. From that moment on, Angela was working from a different set of priorities.

She doesn't say anything to her parents. She doesn't really know how their liberal politics will stand up to the fact that their only daughter is going out with—or seeing, as her mum always calls it—a tall Asian boy from Uganda, fleeing with his family from Idi Amin's excesses. So she says nothing and hopes no-one will see them together on the bus and tell tales.

But she can't keep her secret from everyone. She's been good friends with Cathy since they met at nursery years ago. Angela and Cathy share lots of things, apart from secrets, including notes they've made about their latest science projects, lipsticks and the occasional item of clothing that's "just perfect to go with my new skirt/blouse/jacket." But one thing they don't share is their view on Ahmed.

"I can't understand what you see in him," Cathy says on Saturday morning as the two trawl the local market stalls for something cool, but cheap, to wear that evening. "He's selfish, he's arrogant and he's not very kind."

"He's kind to me," Angela replies, "and he's great to look at."

Cathy wrinkles her nose.

"Oh yes, he's got the looks, I'll give you that. And doesn't he know it? You should see him when you're not there—preening and showing off in front of all the other girls."

But Angela isn't listening. She knows Ahmed better than Cathy does—or anyone else for that matter.

At that point, the two girls both spot a lime green mini dress and dive towards it. Laughing, they tussle over who will try it on first and then, when the stall holder offers them a second identical dress, so they can have one each, decide with the fickleness of youth they don't want it after all. The discussion about Ahmed is forgotten and Angela doesn't think of it again until the two friends arrive at the disco that night.

Ahmed's sister goes to the private academy on the other side of Newton Abbot. Angela tells her parents she's taking a sleepover with Cathy; her friend's parents are less strict about what their daughter does on a Saturday night. They have the evening to themselves and don't have to worry about getting home for a particular time.

The minute Angela walks through the door, she realises she's made a mistake—or maybe more than one. For a start, the girls at this exclusive school don't look as though they would be at home in a two-up, two-down. In fact, they probably have no idea what that is. Their clothes are elegant, cool and very, very expensive.

"I'm glad we didn't go for those little lime green numbers," whispers Cathy. Angela can only nod dumbly.

She eagerly scans the crowds of young people thronging the dance floor. Finally, she sees Ahmed. He's not dancing. He's not at the bar, buying drinks. Nor is he at the door waiting for her to arrive.

Ahmed is sitting in one of the alcoves at the side of the dance floor. He has one elegant girl draped across his shoulder. Four more similarly dressed young women are arranged around him. All five appear to be hanging on every word. As he talks, his eyes are scanning the crowd. Angela knows he sees her, but apart from a slight stiffening of his frame and a touch of frost in his smile, he shows no sign of being aware she's there.

Angela is about to walk across to the alcove when Cathy grabs her arm.

"Don't you dare!" she hisses. "Let's play him at his own game." She nods towards a couple of young guys strolling towards them from the other side of the room. One is tall and blond; the other has shaggy sandy-coloured hair and is of medium height. Both wear leather jackets and denim jeans.

"We were just going to have a go at that selfish git over there, keeping all the girls to himself," says the blond, grabbing Cathy's hand.

"Then we saw you ladies walking in," says the sandy-haired one, holding out his hand to Angela, "I'm Ron and this is Ewan. Come on ladies, let's get this party started."

The next couple of hours pass in a haze. At one point, Angela glances across to the alcove and sees Ahmed, alone, staring at her. She gives a little wave of her hand over Ron's shoulder, but he doesn't respond. When she looks again, he's gone.

At the end of the evening, Ron and Ewan see them home and the four swap phone numbers. Maybe they'll meet up again; maybe not. It's all very relaxed and Angela realises she hasn't thought about Ahmed for several hours.

"I didn't want to tell you before, in case it wasn't true," says Cathy, as they lie in the twin beds in her room sipping cocoa and nibbling chocolate biscuits, "but one of the lads told me Ahmed was planning to get his own back on you for standing him up last weekend."

"Well," Angela says, "if that's how he behaves after one little let down, goodness knows what he'd be like if something really serious happened. I guess my dad did me a favour, stopping me from going to the coffee bar."

"That reminds me," says Cathy, "you still haven't bought your dad's birthday present, have you? How do you fancy going over to the Sunday market tomorrow — I mean today — and seeing if there's anything nice there? I seem to remember Ron saying he and Ewan might be there this weekend."

July: The Butcher Who Wanted To Garden

Everyone in Coombesford said Richard Makepeace was an excellent butcher. They all bought their Sunday joints from him: topside, leg of lamb, shoulder of pork, chicken or duck; all sourced locally, killed humanely, butchered with skill and bought fresh on Friday or Saturday. Monday was always a quiet day, as the villagers were eating cold meat with their potatoes and greens; but from Tuesday onwards, there was a constant stream of customers through his door: mince for cottage pie or spaghetti bolognaise, chops, belly for casseroles. Yes, everyone in Coombesford loved their butcher's shop. People came from the surrounding towns and villages as well. Richard Makepeace should have been a really happy man—he was certainly a well-off man—but he wasn't content. For Richard Makepeace didn't really want to be a butcher. He wanted to be a gardener.

The Makepeace family had been market gardeners for three generations. His great grandfather bought a smallholding in the Teign Valley back in the nineteenth century and for more than a hundred years they grew potatoes, cabbages, beans and peas that were the talk of the county. They took most of their produce to the weekly markets in Newton Abbot, but they would always sell you a bag of potatoes or a couple of leeks from the back door of their cottage. And if they knew a family was hard up, or someone was ill and unable to work, a basket of vegetables often appeared on the doorstep overnight.

Richard's father used to take him with him when he went out to weed the rows of carrots or pick the beans; but the family's green fingers, hallmark of previous generations, totally passed Richard by. He was too heavy-handed to pull up weeds without yanking out the tender feather-leaved carrots as well. He wasn't light enough on his feet to move among the rows of potatoes without treading on the plants—and on the one occasion his father left him to tend the tomatoes while his parents went to visit a sick relative, he over-watered them so the leaves turned yellow and half the plants rotted away.

"It's no good, son," his father said to him when it was time for him to leave school, "if we leave the market garden to you, it'll be gone within a couple of years. Your brothers can look after the family business; I think we need to find you a different trade." And that was when they saw the notice in the local newspaper for an apprentice butcher. Richard took the job, flourished and became the best butcher in the county.

But he never forgot he should have been a gardener not a butcher. His brothers were doing really well; the red and orange striped vans were a common sight across the county, and many of the people who ate Richard's meat, would accompany it with Makepeace vegetables. The brothers all got on well, and there was a fair bit of cross-marketing done between the two businesses. Richard knew he would never be a market gardener, but he would have loved to serve up a plate of food one day that was all his: meat from the shop and vegetables from his garden.

Not that he actually had a garden. Living in the flat over the shop in a converted barn, all he had was a sunny patch of concrete that he filled with pots of forgiving geraniums every spring. Then, one day he got a call from the Parish Clerk, telling him there was an allotment available. He'd been on the waiting list so long, he'd forgotten all about it. Rushing over to her office at the end of that day, he signed the paper, paid his first year's rent and suddenly, he was a gardener—well, in name anyway.

From that day onwards, Richard spent all his spare time on the allotment. He hurried over on summer evenings, when the long days gave him time to work; and every Sunday he spent a few happy hours digging and planting. And finally he managed to grow a couple of broad bean plants, keeping them alive long enough for the pods to mature and produce something worth cooking.

For the first few months, Richard was happy. Then he started looking at the other allotments around him. As the season progressed, their output increased far more than his. In particular, he noticed the one next to his was superb. Everything was neat and tidy; there were more varieties than on any of the other allotments; and the vegetables were bigger and shinier that everyone's—especially Richard's.

"I'd love to know his secret," Richard moaned to the Parish Clerk when she dropped by for her meat order one day and asked him how he was getting on. "I never see him working on the plot, so I guess he's retired and does everything during the day."

Claire Harford had been Parish Clerk in Coombesford for a couple of years, and Richard liked the look of her from the start, but had been too shy to talk to her before. Now they had a topic of conversation. Claire took to popping in several times a week and they would discuss what he was planting, how he was treating the plants and what he needed to do next. Richard began to obsess about 'the plot next door' and the joy of gardening started to dim ever so slightly.

"I think it's because I've only got a few hours free to do things," he said to Claire one day when the shop was quiet and he'd made them both a cup of tea.

"I could give you a hand if you like," she said. He looked at her in surprise.

"I didn't know you were into gardening," he replied. She told him all about the love of the soil her father had instilled in her when she was growing up.

"I've never forgotten the tips he gave me," she said, "and it would be great to be able to pass them on to someone— to share them with another gardener." Although Richard knew she was just being nice, he was thrilled to be described as a gardener.

"Well, if you've got time, it would be wonderful," he said. "Maybe you would like to join me on Sunday morning."

And so the pattern was established. Richard collected Claire from her cottage just outside the village and they drove to the allotments together. They worked side by side for several hours; she would suggest ways of planting, methods of pest control, the best arrangement of rows to catch the sun. One day, Richard suggested they go to The Falls for lunch afterwards and that became a regular pattern too.

Over the rest of the summer, Richard's gardening skills developed a treat. He learned not to be afraid of the plants. He was able to distinguish between a weed and a seedling; he learned how to prune raspberries so they would fruit heavily the following season. His potatoes started to flourish; his beans grew tall and twined beautifully around the wigwams of canes; his pea plants were sturdy.

Occasionally, on a Wednesday afternoon, Claire and Richard would visit stately homes and other properties in the county with gardens open to the public. They took ideas from what they saw and tried to incorporate them into Richard's allotment.

"Why don't you try putting a few flowers in," Annie suggested one day. "All the best kitchen gardens have a row of sweet peas or chrysanths growing in them; flowers for the big house, usually."

So, Richard added a few flowers the following year and was delighted to see them growing well, flourishing in fact. He became almost more interested in flowers than in vegetables—and Claire's suggestions spurred him on to better and more colourful things.

But if he was completely honest, the allotment next door still looked better kept and more productive than his. The beans had more flowers and therefore more runners; the potatoes stood even taller than his, and probably yielded more tubers; and as for the marrows, they were huge. He'd never seen such specimens.

"It's really intriguing; how does he manage to get everything so big?" he said to Claire over a pint and lunch one Sunday.

"Why don't you ask him," said Claire in what Richard thought was a rather frosty voice.

"Because I never see him! Every time I go up there, I can see signs that he's been around: a row of beetroot weeded; wigwams erected; compost bin topped up or turned; but he's never there."

"And what about the other allotment owners? What do they say?"

"Well, they just tell me it's an old family; been around for a long time—a bit like the Makepeace family, someone said—but no-one can tell me anything about the current owner. But one day, I'll find out," he said. "I've got a day off next weekend, what with the Bank Holiday, so I'm going to spend every minute of daylight up there. He'll have to show his face sometime."

But the owner of the neighbouring allotment didn't appear once throughout the long weekend. Richard was so frustrated. He had to know the secret of his neighbour's success.

Then one day he saw a poster for the Coombesford Garden and Produce Show. It was being held in the Village Hall the following weekend—and there were classes for all sorts of vegetables. Including marrows!

"Got him!" Richard said as soon as Claire walked into the shop that day. She'd taken to bringing her packed lunch in and eating it in the back room with him when the shop was empty.

On the morning of the show, Richard was delighted to see a massive marrow taking pride of place on the display table. He could hardly wait for the afternoon to see who the grower was. He was sure there wouldn't be anything to compete with it, and he was right. When he walked back into the hall after lunch — a nice steak pie in the pub with Claire — his eyes were immediately drawn to the red certificate with 'First Prize' on it, which was propped up against the marrow. He dashed across to look closely, but was disappointed to see the exhibitor's name was missing. He'd have to wait for the prize-giving ceremony.

Just then, one of the judges strolled past and clapped Richard on the back. "Well done, old boy. I see the green fingers have finally appeared," he said, pointing to a table at the other end of the room. Richard walked over to look and stopped in amazement. The flower table was a riot of colour—and there in the middle, with the red winner's certificate next to it, was a vase of his copper chrysanths.

"I told you they were good," said a quiet voice in his ear. Claire was standing next to him with a huge smile on her face. "You were so concerned about those blessed vegetables next door; you ignored what was obvious to me. You have a talent for flowers. So I entered yours—and you won."

When the Chairman of the Society called everyone to order for the prize-giving, Richard took his cup and cheque to great applause, then watched in amazement as Claire went up to receive the prize for the best marrow and several other classes of vegetable as well.

"You were so convinced it was a man who owned that plot; I didn't want to disabuse you. And it was the only way I could think of to get your attention," she said, taking his hand. "You're a hard man to get to know, Richard

Makepeace."

Now, every Sunday, Richard and Claire Makepeace eat lunch in their little cottage on the edge of the village. He supplies the meat and she supplies the vegetables. And on the table will always be a huge vase of flowers.

But Richard secretly still hankers after growing a bigger marrow than his wife's.

August: A Change Of Heart

"To be honest with you—and I bet that's not something you thought you'd hear a politician say—I was beginning to think maybe a career in the church would have been a better option."

Jeremy Fortesque-Smythe was addressing the Annual Dinner of the Coombesford and District Golf Club. They'd asked him to speak about his famous change of heart, which cost him his Ministerial career, but made him a hero in his home county. "However, I'd bullied my younger brother down that road and two potential archbishops in the family was one too many." There were polite chuckles around the room. "So, I went into law instead and from there, naturally enough, into politics."

"As Conservative MP for Devon South-East, I'd been happy on the opposition back benches, sniping at the poor saps on the other side of the House." He didn't mention the long weekends back home; the first-class travel; expense account; drinks on the 3:40pm from Paddington to Exeter, but his wistful smile told its own story. Life had certainly been good.

"Then came that day in May 2010, when our lives turned

upside down. Now we were in charge; we got the blame for everything," and to make things worse, his old school-mate David had promoted him to the front bench, with a health portfolio requiring some tough decisions. "Yes, the church definitely looked like a better option at that point." The laughter swelled sympathetically.

"It had been a hard week. I'd had to announce hospital closures in several cities, including our own dear County General. I'd come home early on the Friday in order to meet with a constituent." He'd been relaxing over dinner in an exclusive, well-hidden restaurant on the edge of Dartmoor. His companion for the evening had driven herself home. He'd hoped for an invitation to join her. However, none was forthcoming, and Jeremy wasn't one to force the issue.

The *maître d'* had looked slightly askance when he realised Jeremy was going to drive himself home but was far too well-trained to make a comment—for which Jeremy thanked him with an extra-large tip. With all the late-night sessions in the bar at the Palace of Westminster, he found his tolerance to alcohol had risen considerably of late.

"As I drove away from the restaurant, the beech trees along the drive leaned in towards me, waving me on my way." By the time he'd passed through Moretonhampstead, the gentle waves had turned into agitation. The sky was banked with cloud. There was no sign of the moon and stars that had shone so brilliantly when he'd started the journey. In the distance, he could hear thunder rumbling over the purr of the engine.

"As I drove along one of the single-track sections, I was blinded by a fork of lightning, then another and another. The third one was right in front of the car and as it hit a tree, the trunk cracked apart." In slow motion, Jeremy had watched a branch fly towards his windscreen. He'd wrenched the wheel, pulled sideways to avoid the hurtling debris, and collided with the bank at the side of the narrow road. There was a crash of glass, a moment of terrific pain— then silence in the darkness, apart from the noise of the storm.

"When I came to, I was pinned behind the steering wheel. I managed to reach into my pocket for my Blackberry." Raising the handset towards his face, he'd groaned when he saw the signal indicator was missing. "I was alone, on an empty road on Dartmoor, behind the wheel of a smashed-up Jag—and my phone was dead." The laughter had stopped now.

Oliver Williams had been on duty for eighteen hours and wasn't sure he should ride his motorcycle across the moors in the dark. But he'd had such a tough day, he just wanted to get back to Sally. He didn't know how he was going to tell her about the closure. They'd only just moved down from Lincoln, and she was so happy here. It would be difficult finding another job, but there was no way they could afford to move again. He'd have to take anything he could until the right job came along.

Slowing down at the approach to a tight bend, he saw glass shards strewn across the road, reflected in his headlights. Then he spotted the car. It was a 1960s Jaguar Mark II featuring the powerful XK twin cam in a classic British exterior, his subconscious told him, dragging up the text from the back of the cigarette cards he'd studied for hours as a child. Only this one wasn't looking classic at all. It was lying at an angle against the bank, half blocking the road, surrounded by fallen branches. A tree leaned drunkenly towards it, as though checking if everything was okay.

As Oliver wheeled his motorbike closer, his headlights illuminated the face of a man trapped behind the crumpled dashboard. His eyes were closed. Blood streaked the cheeks of his strained white face. Oliver realised it was a face he knew. Just a few hours ago, he and his colleagues had watched Sky News in the Relatives' Room. They'd known an announcement was coming; they'd hoped it wouldn't affect them—but it had really surprised no one to hear

South Devon County General Hospital was at the top of the list for closure.

Oliver stood and looked down for a long moment at this man who'd destroyed his happiness, options racing through his mind.

I could get on my bike and ride away—no one would ever know I'd been here. But then Fortesque-Smythe might die.

Well, if he does, will it matter? There'd be one less politician to make a mess of other people's lives.

Or I could hold him prisoner until he changed his mind—my Kathy Bates to his James Caan. And I wouldn't even have to tie him down; the steering wheel's done that for me already.

Or I could just sit with him and see what happens— leave it up to fate.

At that moment, Fortesque-Smythe opened his eyes and gave a start when he saw the young man staring down at him.

"Help me," he murmured.

Oliver's moment of indecision was over. His training and upbringing kicked in.

"Hold on, mate," he said, pulling a phone out of his pocket and grimacing at the missing signal indicator. "I'll need to nip to the top of the hill to get better reception. I'll be right back."

"I have to admit, when I first saw him leaning over me, in head-to-toe black leather, I thought it was the Grim Reaper coming to collect me." Jeremy had told this story many times before and knew how to make this moment seem dramatic, "But it was a young paramedic from County General heading home. He stayed with me until the ambulance came and popped in to see me the next day when his shift was over."

After two days in hospital, Jeremy had been declared out of danger and was transferred to Holmwood Nursing Home for a further eight days of convalescence. Finally discharged, he'd phoned County General and left a message for Oliver, inviting him and Sally to dine with him. There had been no response.

"I had my mail sent down from Westminster as soon as my doctor said I could start working again. The first delivery included an anonymous packet containing an annotated map of Devon. The sender had put a cross on the road where he'd had his accident and then circled the site of County General. Across the top of the map in red pen were the words: good job we were still there, wasn't it Minister? Jeremy paused, slipped his notes back into his pocket and smiled at his audience. "And the rest, as they say, is history."

September: Chasing Stars With A Butterfly Net

After the funeral, Amy's grandparents took her to live with them on the farm. Clambering down from the back of the battered, muddy Land Rover, her gaze was drawn to the wide patch of light making a path from her feet, across the yard and through the field towards the horizon where a creamy cratered moon stared down on her. She leaned backwards against the vehicle and gasped as she slowly took in the display above her head. Orion's Belt, the Plough, the Great Bear plus many others she couldn't name; and threading through them all, the glowing arch of the Milky Way. As a well-educated teenager with an interest in science, she recognised these phenomena from the books she'd read and the television programmes she'd watched with her parents. But as a city girl visiting the Coombesford countryside for the first time in many years, this was a whole new experience.

"Do you think they're up there somewhere, Gramps?" she asked, her voice breaking and the tears she'd held back on the long drive from London finally beginning to slide down her cheeks. Her grandfather sighed and stood for a long time with his arm around her shoulder before speaking.

She was beginning to think he hadn't heard her question.

"I don't know, poppet," he said finally, "maybe they are. You know, in ancient times," he continued, "they used to believe that every person on earth is represented by a star. When Fate decides your time is up, she snips the thread anchoring the star in place in the heavens."

"And the star goes out?"

"Well, maybe, but only after making its way spectacularly to the afterlife." He squeezed her shoulders and bent to wipe the tears from her cheeks. "Come child, let's go in. Tomorrow night, I'll take you to watch their final journey."

"Nanny, are you sure you don't want to come with us?" Amy said the next evening as she and her grandfather collected together blankets, torches and a flask of hot chocolate.

"Good gracious no, child," laughed her grandmother, "My star-gazing days are over. I'll just settle down with my new Dick Francis until you get back."

The young girl and the old man walked across the field and threw down their blankets on a clear piece of grass next to the pond. Switching off the torches, they lay flat on their backs and waited for the show to begin.

Amy knew shooting stars were really meteors, small particles of debris burning up as they pass through Earth's atmosphere. But right now, she didn't need the science or the truth. She needed a way to connect with her parents, snatched from her suddenly, shockingly, by a careless driver, while she was at a friend's birthday party.

"They go so quickly," she whispered. "If only I could hold on to one of them."

As the Perseids meteor shower fizzed and crackled above her head, she tried closing her eyes, capturing the images, but although the stars flickered briefly against her closed lids, they soon disappeared.

"The Greeks believed a shooting star was good luck," said her grandfather. "Maybe we should see if we could track one, see where it falls."

"Or better still, catch it in mid-flight," laughed Amy. Suddenly, she sat bolt upright. "Gramps, I've got an idea! Can we come back tomorrow?"

When the pair left the farmyard for their starry theatre the next evening, Amy had an old butterfly net tucked under her arm. As they lay watching the display, she tried to wrap the net around each of the fiery trails. Her head told her it was an impossibility, but part of her still had to keep trying; the part of her that wanted to believe if she could catch her parents' stars she would be able to keep them with her a bit longer.

"No, that was someone else," she would whisper each time she missed. "When it's you, I'll know."

Amy didn't catch her shooting star that night, nor any night that week. As August gave way to September, she started at her new school and star-gazing was replaced, at her grandmother's insistence, with homework and early nights. As time passed, the hurt became less of a sharp knife in her stomach and more like a dull ache that could be ignored most of the time.

Every year, in the middle of August, Amy and Gramps would cross the field and lie staring at the stars. She never really gave up the hope that she would catch a star, but as she grew older, she swapped the butterfly net for a camera. Even when she left the farm to travel the world, taking pictures of other places, other constellations, she still tried to return in August, to share a week of star-gazing with the old man, especially after her grandmother passed away.

But this year, it was too late. She'd got the call while she was on a photo shoot in Kenya. A heart attack, a short, sharp shock and it was all over. Standing at the graveside where her beloved Gramps was now reunited with his wife, Amy smiled through her tears.

"I guess you'll have a ringside seat at the show this year

Gramps," she said, "and no doubt Nanny will be keeping you company once more. But don't worry, I won't be alone either. I've brought someone with me; I think you'd like him." Then, dropping her flowers on the grave, she turned away to where her new boyfriend, Ian, stood waiting for her. He was an astronomer; they'd met when she'd attended a lecture he'd given on The Myths and Realities of Shooting Stars.

Late that night, Amy and Ian left the farm she now owned, carrying blankets, torches and hot chocolate. They crossed the field to lie under the stars and say farewell to Gramps. And for one last time, Amy had a butterfly net tucked under her arm.

October: Beating Michael Jacobson

"It's mine, Michael Jacobson, all mine. And there's nothing you can do about it!" I mutter as I stroll into the kitchen, nose twitching at the warm aroma.

It's been another busy year for the Coombesford Garden and Produce Society. At the Spring Show, Michael came first in three classes, and I took the other two. The Summer Show was a tie; we won one class each, the third going to a recent newcomer to the village. She isn't in the running for the overall trophy this year, but she'll need watching next time around.

Now we're on the final stretch: autumn fruits and speciality cooking. Neither Michael nor I have any fruit trees and he doesn't bake, so with luck, I'm going to top the points table. And about time too! He's had it his own way far too long.

But as I peer through the glass at the splodge of gunk flowing down the side of the dish, I realise I might be counting my meringues before they're hatched.

Pulling the mess out of the oven, I throw it into the sink in disgust. The tray from the bottom shelf follows it. I grab the entry form from behind the clock and cross the kitchen to the freezer that doubles as our notice board. My score-sheet is held in place by magnets depicting the Eiffel Tower, the Washington Memorial, and Shaggies Dog Grooming Parlour in Newton Abbot.

I make rapid calculations, and double check my figures. If my lemon meringue doesn't take at least third place, I've no chance of beating Michael. And as he might do well in the jams and pickles section, I really need a second to be certain of beating him. I'd been quietly confident of first place—but now my plans are in ruins.

It's nine fifteen, and the entries need to be in by two; there's just time to start again. Yanking open the fridge door, I grab the butter and eggs. I turn to the vegetable rack for the lemons—and that's when I remember the previous evening: a long day in the surgery for Paul; a stressful day with a sick dog in the kennels for me; late night supper of salmon and cream cheese bagels *with lemon juice*, washed down with gin and tonics *with slices of lemon*. I'll have to go shopping before I can start cooking again. Luckily, it takes just a minute or two to pop up the road to the Village Store. I grab my purse and run.

There's one other person in the shop when I get there, an elderly lady. She looks familiar, although I can't quite place her, and I smile as I stretch past her for some lemons from the carefully stacked display.

"Don't they remind you of Italian summers?" she says. "I don't think we've met. I'm Caroline Skelton; I've just bought Farm Cottage." Then I remember where I've seen her. She's the newcomer who won the class at the Summer Show.

"Annabel," I say, "Annabel Goodwin. Yes they do—but they're for a very English recipe this time." Then I stop and look at her closely. "Are you entering any of the classes in the show?" She laughs and shakes her head.

"No, not this time," she says, "I'm waiting for my kitchen to be finished. I'll be ready to compete next year." She takes a newspaper from the pile and strolls towards the counter. Looking over her shoulder, she carries on. "I take it you're entering the pie class. You're leaving it a bit late aren't you?" I sigh and nod my head.

"You're so right. In fact, I wouldn't bother if I wasn't finally so close to beating Michael Jacobson," I admit.

And before I have time to think, I'm telling a total stranger all about the competition; how Michael wins the trophy every year; my determination to beat him this time; and how it was all going so well—until I opened the oven— and then found there were no more lemons in the rack.

"But I wasn't going to give up as easily as that," I say, "so here I am and now I'm going back to my kitchen to do it again—and this time, it's got to be right!"

"You know, I've always been a dab hand at meringues," Caroline says. "Would you like some tips?"

"That would be great," I reply. "Have you got time for a coffee?"

"My dear, I have all the time in the world," she says, picking up her basket. "Lead the way. And you can tell me why it's so important to beat this Michael Jacobson."

"Well, to begin with, he's a bully—and so sure of himself. Apparently, he was born around here, although he lived away for a long time."

"And now he's back...?"

"He arrived a year or so after we moved in—must be ten years back—and ever since, he's been bossing everyone around, telling us how we can improve the place and so on."

"Hmm, he certainly sounds a bit over-bearing."

"Paul, that's my husband by the way, calls him 'The Village King'!"

"And you think beating him to the trophy's going to make him change his behaviour, do you?" she asks gently. I blush.

"I doubt if anything's going to do that—but I would love to let him see he can't have everything his own way." I hold my kitchen door open and usher her in. "I suppose you think that's really childish, don't you?"

"Of course it is, dear," she smiles, "but if we can't exercise our inner child occasionally, the world would be a much duller place, wouldn't it?" She puts down her basket and pushes up her sleeves. "Right, point me in the direction of the coffee, while you make a start on the pastry." She points to the clock; I'm running out of time.

As Caroline bustles around, filling the kettle, finding the mugs, and pouring coffee into the jug, she keeps up a stream of tips for the perfect pie. As a child, I made pastry for the jam tarts with my mother every Sunday, but we'd never used lard with the butter, to make it crisper. Nor did I usually bake the case blind before filling it; but that's what we do now, while I make the lemon sauce, thicker than last time, so it will set more quickly.

Next we work on the meringue. Caroline tells me to make sure the bowl is spotless; to bring the eggs to room temperature before whipping them; and to use more egg whites than the book suggests. I always follow recipes slavishly, so am wary about this.

"Oh fiddlesticks," she says, "recipes are only for guidance."

Finally, we ignore the cooking instructions, and reduce the temperature from gas mark 6 to gas mark 1. There will be just enough time to bake the pie this way before I have to get my entry in.

"It takes longer this way, but it's a dryer, crisper meringue," she assures me.

I carry my pie across the green and into the Village Hall minutes before the deadline. The meringue is piled four inches high above the top of the flan dish. It's a pale coffee brown colour, dry as a biscuit and when I cut the slice for the judges, it cracks like ice on a river when the thaw sets in. The sauce is canary yellow, enhanced by the extra egg yolks Caroline encouraged me to use. The pastry is thin, brittle, and dry. It's the best pie I've ever baked.

And the judges obviously agree. When the doors open

at 4pm, there's the red certificate, proclaiming 'First Prize', next to my entry. Added to the second prizes for mustard pickle and blackberry jelly, I'm home and dry.

To give him his due, Michael Jacobson is the first to shake my hand after the trophy presentation.

"Well done, Annabel," he says. "I can see I'll need some lessons in baking if I'm to get my trophy back next year." Then he turns and indicates a small figure standing just behind him. "I don't think you've met my mother-in-law, have you? She's just moved back to the village after living abroad for years."

In the split second before she moves fully into view, I know; I just know!

"Hello my dear," she says, eyes twinkling, "I'm Caroline. Let me add my congratulations to Michael's".

As the pair leave the hall a few minutes later, my new friend looks back and places a finger to her lips. I know my secret is safe. But I also know the newest member of the village is certainly going to take some watching. There will be three of us after the trophy next year—and somehow, I don't think I'm going to win the pie-making class again!

November: A Day To Remember

Will she talk to me today? I ask myself the same question every blessed year, and it's always the same answer. Not this time. Maybe next year. But I'm going, as I do every time, to see if I can see her. See if she's ready.

This is an important day, so it's dress uniform. Trousers pressed with a sharp crease front and back. Tunic done up to the neck, all the buttons shining brightly—and so they should. I've spent so long polishing them, waiting for this day to come. Cap brushed and neatly folded; held in place by the epaulette until it's time to wear it. Boots polished so brightly I really can see my face in the toe-caps. A bit of spit and polish my old dad used to call it; elbow-grease was my mum's phrase. I won't even say what the Sergeant Major called it, but it had an effect on us lads; our boots always shone—except when they were covered with mud, of course. Although, even then, you could sometimes see some remnants of the hard work. I remember when young Billy copped it. We dragged him through the mud, back into the trench and propped him up against the wall, out of the line of fire. He was covered in mud from head to toe, but his toecaps were peeping through, still sparkling. I thought at the time he'd be pleased about that. He wouldn't want to go into heaven with muddy boots.

I could have done with getting my hair cut; it's starting to look a bit long for an army lad. But it's too late. I'll grease it down and hope it stays in place. She wouldn't like to see me looking untidy, would she?

Okay, that's it; ready to go. Not going to need my rifle today; there won't be any enemy around, that's for sure. Unless you count Tommy, the butcher's boy. He never liked me; we were real enemies when we were kids. But he's not been the same since that gas attack. I don't think he's going to give me any trouble this time.

I always love this service. Arriving at the church, seeing the dignitaries assemble. A bit like muster back at the camp. Apart from the fact they're all in their Sunday best, of course; and if they heard a shot fired, they'd probably all run a mile. Oh look, there's the leader of the council; he's the one with the long gold chain weighing him down. Actually, the chain itself is quite light, I understand, but the office seems to be taking its toll on him. So many people to look after, to answer to, to keep happy. And worse still, all those names to read out this morning. So many names; every family in the village seems to have lost someone. And when the mayor gets to his own family, you can hear the little choke in his voice.

And here comes the district councillor, looking dapper as usual. I always think gold-rimmed glasses give one a look of dignity. He's looking around a lot; checking to see if the press has arrived, I expect. I never knew a man quite so keen on getting his name in the local paper. You can always tell whether there's a reporter in a meeting by the number of interventions he makes. And there will always be a controversial one, a slight indiscretion. He may apologise afterwards, but it'll be too late; the comment will be in the reporter's notebook and into the paper the very next week. Not that it makes much difference; tomorrow's chip paper, that's what my old mum used to call the Weekly Herald; that old rag was what my dad called it.

It's always such a moving service. The choir lead the procession up the aisle; first the young boy with the cross — they only bring that out on special occasions; then the sopranos and altos, followed by the tenors and basses. They look right formal in their maroon cassocks with crisp white surpluses over the top, each with a bright red poppy pinned to the shoulder. Next comes the vicar; he always looks good in his robes. Mind you when you're that tall and thin, you tend to look good in anything. Then come the regimental colours and the standards for the children's organisations. I guess that's why the pews are so full this week. There's nothing like involving a child in something to guarantee bringing the parents out in force. Although some of those youngsters could do with a bit of discipline. Those arms aren't very straight, and the cubs' banner is waving about like they're on a sports field rather than in church.

The music's always so stirring today as well. That organist chappie loves the noisy ones. He's best at the Welsh hymns: *Bread of Heaven* is a particular favourite of his. But he makes a great job of *Abide with Me* and *Dear Lord and Father of Mankind*. He even enjoys playing the National Anthem; I suppose the Monarch is as important in Wales as in England.

Well, that's the sermon over; not too long today. I guess the vicar is thinking of all the children in the congregation; doesn't want them wriggling and distracting people. Interesting things he had to say today; I especially liked the bit about the soldier from here who lost his life on active duty and how he'd been awarded a posthumous medal. Nice to hear our efforts are appreciated and recognised here at home, so far away from all the action.

And now we get to the bit that always brings tears to the eyes. The Last Post. No bugler again this year I see; not too common these days — but that young girl with the cornet does a good enough job. The long discordant notes echo through the church. She's playing from the choir gallery at the back, so the sound drifts across people's consciousness without them being able to see the musician. Makes it easy to think we're on a battlefield, or at a graveyard; come to think about it, there's not much difference between those two. The standards are all lowered towards the ground; at least it's clean in the church; they look awful when they trail in the mud.

As the final note dies away, we're straight into the two-minute silence. Even the church clock has been silenced and the only sound is the occasional cry of a baby. Seems appropriate somehow. We're all babies at heart, and I've heard men on the battlefield sob for their mothers. A young woman at the back of the church looks embarrassed and tries to hush her child, which only makes it worse. But if she looked up, she'd see sympathetic smiles all around her. No-one minds the sound of a child—after all, it reminds us that life does go on, no matter what shitty things it might throw at us along the way.

Even some of the older members of the congregation start to shuffle a bit towards the end. Two minutes doesn't sound very long, but it's one hundred and twenty seconds, which seems to go on forever when you can't see the clock and don't know how fast time is moving. I see one of the members of the choir glancing surreptitiously up at the cornet player, waiting for her to indicate the time is up. And here she goes: instrument to her lips, a burst of sound, we're into Reveille and the standards shoot upright once more, before being deposited around the altar for the rest of the service.

And so, we pray, we put money on the collection plate, we pray some more, and we sing another hymn. Then it's over and we leave the church to process to the War Memorial for the remainder of the ceremony. I'm not sure if I'm going to follow them any further. I've heard the names read out before; hell, I was there with many of them at the end. I don't need to hear their names to remember their faces, their agony, or their final words: "Tell my mother I love her." "Tell Ada I'll never forget her." "Do you think I'll be home in time for Christmas?" Well, we all wanted to know the answer to that one, didn't we? No, I think I'll just sit here in the churchyard and rest awhile.

I looked for her, as I always do, as I have done for many years now. She wouldn't be able to see me, not from where I was standing, but she was easy to pick out once you know what to look for. Tiny she is, not more than five foot one, and dressed completely in black. Of course, lots of people are in black today, or at least in dark sober outfits; even in this day and age, there are a lot of people who know that a mark of respect is still important. But her black is different. It's deeper, more permanent somehow. You feel if some of them went out in the rain, the black would be like cheap dye; it would run away, leaving them in their normal bright colours. But her black is the real deal. She wears an astrakhan coat; you don't see many of those any longer; and a little pill-box hat with a veil. Her gloves are leather as is her bag, which sits, just like Mrs Thatcher's, on one arm, even when she's singing the hymns. She's surrounded by the family. Two sons, both getting on a bit now, plus assorted grandchildren and partners. All here "to support Gran" as I've heard them say many times before. It wouldn't do to let on they came for their own sake, would it? Not in this cynical age, even though I've seen one or two of them sneak out a hanky during the silence. Even that great lump in the drainpipe trousers has been known to sniff a bit more than usual during the Last Post.

The procession's leaving the churchyard now; first the standards, then the choir. The Parish Council, carrying the wreaths they're going to lay, fall in behind them. Then we have the scouts, the guides, cubs and brownies. Finally, the congregation strolls in the winter sunshine across the green to the War Memorial. The road is blocked by police cars, not that there's much traffic about. Most of the cars stop of their own accord: at the eleventh hour, of the eleventh day, of the eleventh month... as a mark of respect.

47

She carries my picture in her locket; I see her clutch it as she leaves the church and joins the procession. Every year, I wonder will she see me; will she come and join me on my bench: not able to participate, but a spectator always. And every year, I find I'm too early. She still remembers, but she cannot see.

Yet this year, as she leaves the churchyard, she pauses, turns, and looks straight at me. I see her smile, a puzzled, questioning smile, before she turns and walks away, leaning on our elder son's arm. Not this year, my love; not yet. But soon; I sense that very soon, you'll not walk away from me. We'll stand hand-in-hand to watch as others walk. And when that day comes, you'll find me waiting here. Faithful as I've always been, these seventy years or more.

December: The Business Man And The Pop Star

Arthur's heart sank as the train pulled into the station. The platform was heaving with festival goers; it was Tuesday, the day after Bank Holiday Monday and even someone who'd been on another planet for the past two weeks and didn't know anything about the annual music festival in the grounds of the county's largest stately home would have been able to work out something had been going on. It wasn't usual to see this quiet seaside station packed with— well, 'hippies' wasn't a word one heard very often these days, but it was the only one Arthur could bring to mind. Groups of young people were leaning against pillars, sprawling across seats, or sitting on the floor. Some were chatting animatedly, and one large group were singing along to a guitar, but most were dozing where they stood, or staring into space. It looked like nobody had slept for several days—and even without being close enough to check, Arthur knew they wouldn't have been too fussed about hygiene at the festival grounds either.

The train remained on the platform for several minutes, while the announcer told "customers" there was a problem with a signal further down the line and they were held up by another train just ahead of them. He apologised for "any inconvenience caused" but it didn't sound as though he meant it. It was more a case of "I've got to sit here on this train and put up with it, so everyone else has to as well."

As the festival goers got on the train, Arthur left his briefcase on the seat next to him and buried his nose in his newspaper. A couple of people slowed as they approached and looked pointedly at him—he could see their reflection in the window—but he ignored them and they moved on to other parts of the train, leaving him with his precious double seat to himself. He'd been doing this journey for years now and no-one's stares had any effect on him. It was a point of honour to maintain the empty seat next to him for as many days as possible. Today would make it twenty-five—nearly a month—and a personal record for him. He smiled to himself and made a mental note to brag to Billy Jones when they got to work the next day.

Just then three things happened at once: the guard blew the whistle, the train gave a lurch as the brakes were released prior to starting off, and the carriage door was yanked open. A tall balding man in jeans and a polo-necked jumper flung himself into the carriage and slammed the door shut, just as the train began to move. He walked straight over to Arthur's seat, picked up the briefcase and dropped it on the table with a "you don't mind do you, mate?" and subsided into the seat with a massive sigh.

Arthur stared at him in consternation. It wasn't that this man had touched his things, although that was sacrilege on a British train. It wasn't that he'd lost his precious double seat and with it his chance to snatch the record off Billy Jones. It wasn't even the fact that this was obviously someone from the festival and therefore not the freshest-smelling passenger with whom to spend a journey. No, it was the fact that Arthur knew this man. He'd spent his teenage years with his picture pinned up on his wall. He'd bought all his records and had once saved up his pocket money for three months to buy a ticket to a concert in

Plymouth. This was Jet Stevens, lead singer of the Granite Elephants, hero of many a 1960s teenager; and therefore always 21 in their eyes. He couldn't be an aging festival goer. It wasn't right—and it was too much of a reminder to Arthur that he was no longer a teenager either.

"God, that was terrible." The words ricocheted around the compartment. Arthur looked up from his newspaper— he'd been staring at it unseeingly, trying to decide whether to speak to this living legend or to ignore him. His inclination was leaning towards the latter, but Jet had taken the decision out of his hands.

"What, the station? Yes, it's the festival you know." Arthur groaned inwardly; how could he try to tell Jet Stevens about a music festival?

"No, not the station, man; I could handle the station. I'm talking about the festival."

"Oh, right," Arthur murmured.

"It's all my new manager's fault," Jet continued. Arthur looked around wildly. Everyone else was studiously avoiding his eyes, but he was fairly sure they were all listening intently. "I told him it was a mistake booking me a slot. But would he listen? No he wouldn't!" Arthur cleared his throat and shook his newspaper irritably, but his companion carried on regardless. "I told him they wouldn't have heard of me—and I was right."

"But everyone's heard of you." The words were out of Arthur's mouth before he could stop them. "You're Jet Stevens."

Jet swivelled in his seat and stared at Arthur open-mouthed.

"Fancy a suit like you knowing who I am."

"Are you kidding? I've got every one of your albums— even that odd one you did during your punk phase—and I've seen you play live many times over the years." He glanced down at his suit and briefcase and smiled ruefully, "I didn't always dress like this, you know."

"Man, I could have done with you at the festival," said

Jet, "and a few of your friends as well. They put me on during the day—late morning, in fact. Half the kids were still in bed and those that were up and about seemed more interested in finding some breakfast than listening to my music. Someone told me they were 'like really, really tired'!"

"Not like the Isle of Wight '69 then?"

"You were there?" Arthur nodded, "Wow, yeah, that was some gig. I reckon there was so much dope being smoked there, the seagulls must have been stoned for a week after we'd left."

"Not to mention the old girls on the sea-front."

"Right! The ones that tutted every time we walked past. I don't think they appreciated our music at all, did they?"

"And they didn't like you here, either?"

"Well, if I'm honest, the reception wasn't too bad once I'd got started. They clapped politely when I came on, but were cheering by the time I finished. I even heard one or two brave souls singing along with the chorus of *Brighton Belle*."

"Oh, I've done that once or twice myself. *Brighton Belle, you can go to hell*"

"*I'm off to see the world*" Jet joined in.

Arthur looked around, a bit embarrassed at being caught singing on the 17:37 from Exeter St David but noticed the few people who did meet his eye (it was that sort of train) were actually grinning and one woman at the other end of the compartment was also singing along. Arthur suddenly didn't feel like a bank manager; he was right back to his student days.

"I saw you perform that live in Regent's Park," he said. Jet looked confused, but Arthur nodded confirmation. "I was at Bedford College. We used to have live bands on stage every Sunday. I saw Elkie Brooks when she was singing with Vinegar Joe; my namesake Arthur Brown with his Crazy World; I even saw Hawkwind one night—no, I tell a lie; that was at one of the University College gigs. I bopped to *Tiger Feet* when Mud came to play at our Christmas Party; and I was there when you guys did your surprise appearance at the charity gig. I hadn't wanted to go; I was working for an exam the following week but my flat mates convinced me to pop out for a quick pint—and I was so glad I did."

"Oh yes, I'd forgotten that. Someone had to drop out and they asked us at the last minute. I seem to remember we raised a lot of money that evening."

"And then, when you did the *Brighton Belle* tour, I skipped lectures to queue for tickets. They went on sale in the Virgin Store on Oxford Street at four o'clock in the afternoon and we'd been there since six in the morning. Got told off by a policeman for sitting on the pavement; apparently we were making the place look untidy! But it was worth it—and we got ace seats."

"Happy days." Jet seemed to relax. Arthur told him he hadn't realised the Granite Elephants were still performing live.

"We're not; we've not been on stage all together since the big bust-up in 1983, although three of us got together and did a bit of a tribute when Antony died. Joey plays with another band now, and Vinnie's pretty much retired—his health's not good, I'm afraid." He paused and they paid silent tribute to missing band members. "It's just me that wanted to get back on the road, really. But I'm not sure this new manager of mine is going to work out."

"Not getting you enough work?"

"No, quite the opposite. It was him that got me the festival gig—but it's not what I want any more. I don't want to play big stadia or packed festival grounds. I certainly don't want to go on tour—and I'm not interested in going down the celebrity reality show route."

"So we're not going to see you on *Celebrity Big Brother* any time soon then?" Arthur grinned.

"God forbid! No, I just want to perform to small crowds of fans who like my music—like we did in the early days." Jet sighed. "But I guess it's not possible to turn back the clock like that, is it?"

"Well, you could come and play at Coombesford Christmas Fayre for starters," Arthur said.

"Coombesford, where's that?"

"It's a village in the Haldon Hills. We have a Fayre on the first Saturday of December, when we switch on the Christmas Lights. There's mulled wine, mince pies and lots of craft stalls. And we have live music on the village green. I chair the organising committee. It would be great if you'd come and sing for us." Arthur stopped, realising what he'd just suggested. "But I guess that might be too small for you. Forget I mentioned it."

But Jet assured Arthur he thought it was a great idea and once he'd run it past his manager, he'd get back to him. Jet took a copy of Arthur's card.

Arthur assumed that was the last he'd hear from the ageing pop star, but three days later when he got home, his wife was standing on the doorstep waiting for him, her eyes sparkling and a huge grin on her face.

"You'll never guess who I've been chatting to this afternoon," she said as she kissed him and took his briefcase out of his grasp.

And four months later, on a frosty night in December 2003, Jet Stevens of the Granite Elephants sang on Coombesford Green. Arthur and his wife stood at the front of the stage with a crowd of their friends. There was a lot of grey hair in evidence, both on stage and in the audience. But there were no suits and very few ties. And when they all joined in the chorus of *Brighton Belle* at the end of the evening, you could hear them halfway across Devon.

January: Paddy's Pride and Joy

"I knew this was a foolhardy idea," Marian grumbles, pushing a branch out of the way and blowing her fringe from her eyes. "We should just buy three plants and be done with it." She's always been the sensible one, has Marian; which is why it's all the more surprising to see her crouching in the undergrowth with us.

"But it wouldn't be the same, now would it?" hisses Sarah. "Dad never bought anything for the garden if he could help it. And it's all about him, remember?"

"Keep quiet, the two of you!" I lapse into big sister mode. "There's someone coming. We'll get caught if we're not careful."

It had all started with a casual comment during one of our weekly phone calls. We were wondering how to mark our dear departed father's centenary. Sarah suggested we make a donation in his name to his favourite charity. I was leaning towards dedicating a tree in his name. Of course, that would be a fully grown, mature tree, not one we had to plant ourselves; I'm not into digging and planting. The green-fingered gene Dad passed down to his other two daughters seems to have missed me completely. Marian suggested we buy three plants, and remember him privately, rather than with a grand public gesture.

"Or maybe we should just take a penknife and visit one of the National Trust gardens," Sarah said with a laugh. And just like that, the idea was born.

Everyone who knew him believed Dad was as honest as the day was long; although there was the occasional accusation of cheating when we played cards. He never knowingly told a lie—because stories about Santa Claus and the Tooth Fairy don't really count— and he was scrupulous about never taking what didn't belong to him. He was always the first to return extra coins if he was given too much change in a shop.

But he had one weakness. He loved taking plant cuttings—and the riskier the undertaking, the better. Our local park; the flower beds of Mountjoy Manor near our home in Coombesford; Kew Gardens; The Eden Project; and even the Japanese Gardens at the Curragh, which we visited each summer while back home staying with relatives; nowhere was safe when Dad was in cuttings mode. We learned to confiscate his penknife on days out, long before terrorism turned the carrying of knives to an illegal act.

Which is why three, generally law-abiding, middle-aged women find themselves, one Friday in June, creeping towards the rose house in the grounds of this magnificent property, each with a tiny penknife in her pocket. To onlookers, we probably don't look suspicious; after all, the gardens are open to the public and there are plenty of people around. We're just three friends—because sisters can be friends too—out for a stroll. You'd probably have to watch us very closely to notice we're creeping around, hiding behind shrubs or trees every time one of the gardeners comes into view. But if the other two feel anything like I do, their hearts will be thudding, their palms sweaty and they'll be convinced the sign of guilt is written all over their faces.

"We're so going to have to go to Confession after this," mutters Marian.

Our childhood memories abound with warm days spent playing in our back garden on a lawn surrounded by roses. There were blood red ramblers covering the trellis around the edge; delicate peach-coloured standard bushes in the formal flowerbed along the wall; and strongly scented ones whose petals we would collect to press or dry for *pot pourri*. But Dad's favourite was the fuchsia pink, fragrantly scented *Paddy's Joy*.

"My very own pride and joy," he'd call it, looking around expectantly for us to laugh at his wit; and we did—even though we'd heard the saying every year since he'd nicked a cutting from the first bush to be exhibited in a recently-established rose house. He tended that cutting so carefully and we still remember his pride the first time it bloomed.

Now, I push those memories to the back of my mind as we finally reach the rose house and slip inside. We stroll, smelling each specimen, even those with no scent, until the place is empty.

"Quick, while there's no-one around," says Sarah. "They're over here." She whips out her knife, carefully selects a piece from the back of a plant and slices it away. In a flash, her trophy is in a plastic bag, deep in her pocket. Marian follows suit, exclaiming softly as the rose fights back and catches the back of her hand with a vicious thorn.

"You're not making this easy, are you, Dad?" I murmur, looking skywards. And then it's my turn. I step forward, carefully select a shoot, and then pause, glancing back at my more horticulturally-confident sisters for reassurance. They both nod impatiently.

"Hey, what are you doing over there?" The voice, booming around the glasshouse, takes us all by surprise. We were so intent on capturing the cuttings, we didn't realise we were no longer alone. One of the gardeners is standing by the back door, looking suspiciously at us. Sarah and I glance at each other and swallow. Marian pulls herself up to her full five feet four inches and stares at him.

"We're just checking for greenfly, young man," she says in her best schoolmarm voice. Sometimes I feel rather sorry for Marian's pupils, but now I'm glad to hear the note of authority in her speech. "This species is particularly susceptible. But I'm glad to see you've managed to keep them in check here. Well done!" And without glancing at the two of us, she turns and heads for the door. We follow her in a rush.

Back at my house, we calm our nerves with coffee and cake, then arrange to meet on Sunday to visit Dad's grave. The other two discuss the best way to treat their cuttings.

"With a bit of luck, we'll have a flowering plant or two by next year," says Marian.

I can't help feeling I've let the side down by not getting my cutting. Without telling the other two, I head back to the gardens the following day. Once again, I spend ages wandering around, waiting for the rose house to be empty. It isn't easy; being a Saturday, the place is heaving with families. It's after half past four by the time there's a gap in the crowds. The gardeners are all outside—I make sure I check this time—so I slip in through the door, thinking a quick slice is all it will take, and I'll be out of there. And it would have been—except they've been planting the outside beds—and all the bushes of *Paddy's Joy* are gone. While I've spent the afternoon wasting time, dodging school kids and gardeners, I've probably been closer to my goal than I am at this moment.

With a sigh, I leave the rose house and head for the shop. There might be some on sale there—and I reckon I can buy one and take a cutting from that. I know that's not the point of the exercise, but I'm running out of time. In the event, I can't even do that; they don't have any on sale. I'm just about to give up and leave for home when I hear a voice behind me.

"Not looking for greenfly in here, I hope. Our shop manager's very particular about the specimens we give her to sell." It was the gardener from yesterday. He's crept up behind me and is standing there grinning, with his hands on his hips. I can feel myself blushing and as much as I try to find a quick response, nothing comes to mind. I shake my head at him.

"You didn't believe us, did you?"

"Not for one second," he replies, his grin getting bigger, "But I have to give your friend full marks for quick thinking." Then he points towards the cafe. "Come and have coffee while you tell me what you three were really doing."

So, I do. I go for coffee with a complete stranger—and find myself telling him what we were doing—and why. Actually, that's not quite true. I tell him all about our father, Patrick or Paddy to his friends, his love of roses and his penknife exploits. I tell him the next day will be one hundred years since Dad's birth and about the roses that surrounded us throughout our childhood. I don't quite get around to telling him about our own memorial trophies.

"And your father pinched a cutting from *Paddy's Joy* back in the early days after it was just cultivated?" he says. He sounds disapproving, and I wonder for a moment if there might be any retrospective repercussions, but then he starts laughing and admits he often did the same when he was growing up. His family was short of cash and wouldn't let him spend anything on plants, so he had to 'beg, borrow or steal' most of the ones he used to turn a little mud patch behind their house into a garden.

"Would you like to see what we've been working on today?" he asks as we finish our coffee. Then he takes me for a walk around the garden and shows me where they've planted the bushes of *Paddy's Joy*. They're in a lovely new bed, around a stone fountain.

When his phone rings, he says he has to take the call, but he won't be above five minutes. As he disappears around the hedge, I nip onto the flower bed and claim a cutting from a good bushy plant at the back, wrap it up and pop it in my bag. By the time he returns, I've removed my footprint from the soil and am taking pictures of the new feature. I tell him my sisters will love to see it. Then he walks me to the gate, shakes my hand and says to say hello to my sisters the next time I see them. I tell him we'll be getting together tomorrow at the cemetery.

"Well, at least we got two cuttings," says Sarah as we stroll across the grass the following day. "Dad would be proud of us."

"Well, actually, we got more than two," I say. The others stare at me open-mouthed as I tell them all about my adventure. "So, we now have three cuttings to look after in Dad's name," I finish.

Then, as our parents' grave comes into view, we stop in amazement. Sitting in the vase at the base of the headstone are three fragrant, fuchsia pink blooms. There's a card nestling among the stems. I pull it out and feel my eyes prick with tears as I read out loud: "*Paddy's Joy* to bring joy to Paddy's daughters; because even the best of cuttings takes more than a day to bloom."

We start to laugh. And from overhead, I swear I hear someone else laughing with us.

"Happy Birthday, Dad," I whisper.

February: Gingham and Leather

There was a gingham-edged sign hanging on the door handle when I rolled in on Saturday night—well, Sunday morning really—after a session in the student bar: "Quiet please, little princess needs her beauty sleep." Gingham! I dropped it in the nearest bin.

As I opened the door, the smell hit me! Sure, I'd planned to buy an air freshener; but something spicy—not bloody lavender—it smelt like my Gran's hankie. Sneezing, I switched on the light. The figure in the spare bed was so pretty, I felt nauseous. She smiled and waggled her fingers.

"Hi, I'm Cissie. You must be Andrea. Or, if you're not Andrea, what are you doing in my room?" My room! I winced as she giggled.

"It's Andy," I muttered, wishing I'd skipped that last pint. It's hard to have a row with someone when you're bursting for a pee.

"Well, you look like you need your sleep. Nightie, night," she simpered, switching off the light and turning over. After doing the necessary, I stripped in the dark and fell into bed, my last thought: girlie, we're gonna have a serious talk tomorrow morning.

"Hey, sleepy head, wake up! Let's go get breakfast!" I thought it was a bad dream, but the voice nagged at my brain. I pulled my head from under the pillow and squinted at the figure in pink. And when I say pink, I mean really pink. From the Lycra vest and tight leggings to the top-of-the-range running shoes, there was barely a colour in sight that wasn't pink. A band held her blonde curls in place; pink and white gingham.

"What time is it?"

"Almost seven! I've been up ages—had a lovely run around the campus—you must come with me next time."

Seven! On a Sunday! I'll kill her—and no-one would blame me!

Cissie headed for the bathroom. I pulled the covers over my head, but it's difficult to sleep when someone's singing *Edelweiss* in your shower. As she moved on to something about goatherds, I gave up. When she returned, shiny and pinker than ever, I was sitting up wearing my 'serious talk' face.

"Cissie, there's things we've got to agree if we're going to be roommates."

"Yes, I know." She shook her finger and gave one of her little giggles; I ground my teeth. "I hope you won't be in that state every night?"

"No, of course not," I protested. "It was Saturday!" Why was I justifying myself?

"Anyway," she went on, "I'm starving. I went for a walk yesterday evening, waiting for my roomie to come home...," Roomie! "...and I spotted a darling little cafe down by the quay." She pulled on tailored trousers and a spotted blouse and headed for the door. "Sure you won't join me?"

I avoided Cissie for the rest of the day, and when I returned from the bar that evening, she was asleep. The gingham notice was back—it went back in the bin. She was up before me on Monday, although I don't think she sang in the shower. By the time I surfaced, she was gone.

At lunchtime, I was in the canteen with the guys when I heard a giggle and groaned inwardly.

"Room for a little one? I don't know anyone else and I hate eating alone." I didn't move, but the others shuffled along the bench to make room. Cissie put down her lunch—salad, yoghurt and an apple—what else? "I'm Cissie, Andrea's roommate."

Steve gave a little snort and I stamped on his toe.

"It's Andy," I reminded her.

"Oh, but that sounds so masculine," she said with a little shudder. "Andrea's such a pretty name." Steve was openly grinning. Tony held out his hand.

"Hi Cissie, I'm Tony. And this grinning ape is Steve."

That lunchtime was the worst ever. Cissie chattered: how pneumonia made her a late arrival on campus; how she was settling in; and how I'd made her really welcome. I searched for irony in her voice, but her sweet smile never slipped.

"What course are you on, Cissie?" asked Steve.

"American History. I know Andrea's doing mathematics—what about you two?" When she heard the replies: physics and applied biology, she bit her lip. "Gosh you must be brainy. I feel quite humble, with a bunch of scientists." For goodness sake, was she for real? But Tony gave her a grin and Steve sat up straighter.

Thank God she was on a different course. At least I wouldn't be sharing lectures with her.

"Andrea," she said, tapping my arm with pink-tipped nails, "what societies would you suggest I join?"

"I hear the running club's good. And there's DebSoc, if you fancy an argument on a Friday evening."

"But, which ones have you joined?" I gulped and didn't answer; just looked at my watch.

"Come on, it's nearly two! We're gonna be late." As I headed out of the canteen, I heard Cissie's giggle. Glancing back, I saw the guys standing chatting with her.

Even though I avoided spending too much time with my roommate, I was still aware of her presence. Apart from that notice—which I finally left where it was, like a piece of ironic post-modernist Goth art—there were other changes.

The bathroom had seemed such a huge space when I first arrived. I go in for the natural approach to hygiene—soap, shampoo and a big pot of cream to take off my make-up. So, pre-Cissie, I had plenty of space for books, magazines and the radio. But Cissie's got enough stuff to start her own health and beauty course.

"Just the essentials for my beauty routine," I was told when I commented on all the bottles and pots. "And it's not hygienic to keep books in the bathroom," she said, dropping them on my bed. She kept the radio, but now it's tuned to Classic FM, not Kerang!

We shared a kitchenette with Tony and Steve whose room is across the landing from us. I don't go in there often; it's always in a state—or it used to be. Three days after Cissie arrived, she bought not only washing up liquid—we'd been using shampoo—but also a mop with a loop to hang it up; a self-adhesive hook to hang the mop on—and four pairs of rubber gloves! I'm quite into rubber, but generally black and incorporated into an innovative outfit for a Saturday night. It's never shaped like a glove—and never, ever, pink! I never saw anyone wearing them when I popped in to heat up a tin of beans, or leave a dirty mug in the sink—Cissie doesn't like crockery left around the bedroom—but there was always at least one pair drying on the radiator. And the place certainly looked more homely without piles of dirty plates, puddles of spilt coffee, and dollops of tomato sauce.

One evening, Tony, Steve and I were making coffee when Cissie arrived with a piece of paper.

"I've put together a rota," she said. "Now we've got this place straight, it'll be easier to keep clean and we'll only have to do it a couple of times a fortnight each."

"You're expecting to keep this place clean?" I mocked. "Sharing it with these two?" I looked at Tony and Steve for support, but they were frowning at me. There was a silence, and then Cissie cleared her throat.

"Actually, Andrea, it's not the boys who make the mess," she said, stroking my arm like she always did when she had something unpleasant to say.

"Well, who is it, then?" There's no-one else using this kitchen."

"Actually, Andy, it's you," said Steve. I started to protest, but Tony nodded his head. Cissie continued stroking my arm.

"All it takes is a few dirty plates or a couple of used mugs and we have a real mess," she said. "On the other hand, it only takes a few minutes to wash your stuff when you've used it." She walked towards the door, then stopped. "How about we have a little supper party this Saturday; you guys look after starters and dessert—and I'll cook my special lasagne."

After that weekend, Cissie was even more a part of our little group—and sometimes whole days went by without her saying anything that made me cringe.

The term was rapidly coming to an end and everyone was demob happy. Cissie was really, really excited (her words) about going home to Surrey for a traditional festive celebration in the bosom of her loving family (my words). A tiny part of me wished she would invite me, but the thought of matching tablecloths and napkins—"never call them serviettes, Andrea, it's so common"—made me shudder. They'd probably be green and red gingham to match the season. No, I was better off staying where I was. I had some reading to catch up on—and there was the joy of a quick trip home to Coombesford to visit mum and the new stepfather on 25th.

Cissie arrived back on New Year's Eve. The family was in Switzerland for skiing, but she didn't fancy the outdoor pursuits after her illness. We wandered from bar to bar, arriving back at the room around three, singing at the top of our voices.

Then on 3rd January, Justin Overdale arrived and everything changed! Well over six feet tall, his thick black wavy hair was neatly cut and parted, but looked as though it wanted to break loose and grow into a pony tail. And his eyes were vivid green. He wore a smart jacket and pressed chinos. The new University Librarian was so not my type— but I wanted him from the moment he stared into my eyes. Actually, he glanced up as I dropped my returns on the desk, gave a brief, automatic-pilot type smile and went back to checking a list in front of him. But for me, it was enough.

I found myself a strategically-placed table so I could check him out without being too obvious; and that's how I spent most of the day. My study schedule went completely out of the window. I was working on a much more important plan. How could I get myself noticed—and more—by Justin?

By the end of the day, I knew he was polite but cool to everyone. He wasn't gay, as far as I could tell; the few students he engaged with were all female, well-dressed and brunette. At noon, he carried a book and a lunchbox to one of the breakout areas. I didn't want to ruin a beautiful friendship before it started by being accused of stalking, so couldn't get close enough to see whether he was a vegetarian. But that could come later. For now, I needed to make him notice me.

Now, I'm not daft, nor self-deluded. A Goth student with poor eating habits and a natural approach to hygiene would probably not feature high on Justin's list of must-have friends. I needed help with this project. And I knew just the person.

But, it was a lot harder than I expected to get Cissie to help me. When I explained my dilemma, she started laughing. Then she stopped and stared at me.

"You're serious, aren't you?"

"Deadly serious!"

"But Andrea, you hate my style, my clothes and my

eating habits. You even object to my using your proper name!"

"Come on," I muttered, "I've never used the word hate."

"Not in so many words, no; but it's obvious how you feel."

I took a deep breath and tried again.

"Cissie, I'm your roommate. I'm really sorry if I've upset you—but I need your help." I did my big-eyed impression of Puss in Boots—the Shrek version. She held out for a few moments, but I knew she was wavering. Finally, she nodded and grinned at me.

"Okay, Andrea, I'm in. It'll be fun. But," she shook her finger at me, "you've got to do what I say at all times."

Inside, a little voice was asking me what I'd let myself in for.

We spent every spare moment talking, planning and putting 'Project Justin' into action.

Cissie took me to a hair salon where the stylist tutted at my split ends and groaned at the effect of the black dye I'd used for years. He chopped off my pony tail, leaving my hair curling gently around my ears, before tinting it dark chestnut, as close as I could remember to my natural colour, with blonde highlights.

She talked me into having my toenails painted, and only sighed a bit when I chose deep purple with sparkles. I drew the line at having my fingernails done—but promised to stop chewing them.

I agreed to have my legs waxed, but after squealing like a pig throughout the process, I refused point blank to have any other bits done! Even for Justin, there were some places I wouldn't go—and just what is a Brazilian, anyway?

Cissie confiscated my normal college outfits and got me wearing denim. She knew better than suggest I wore her gingham blouses, so we went shopping for shirts and other tops—not frilled ones, but certainly more feminine than usual.

But I came up with the craftiest move all on my own. I'd spotted Justin reading *The Psychology of the Aged*. There was copy in the library, which I borrowed, held on to for a couple of days, then carried to the returns counter, when he was on duty. He glanced at the book, then looked up at me and smiled.

"Hey, I'm reading that at the moment!"

"Really," I drawled, in my best Keira Knightly impersonation, "what a co-incidence."

"What did you think of it?"

"Well, I quite enjoyed the underlying messages, although the author's style is a little dry for my taste. And I totally agree with the assertion that western society is making a mistake in pushing the elderly into homes. We have so much to learn from our more experienced members of society. Personally, I like the extended family model practised in Asia and the Middle East."

I hoped it sounded like I knew what I was talking about. I'd flicked through a couple of pages then Googled a summary on Wikipedia. It seemed to work. He was looking at me intently, nodding in agreement.

"Are you a psychology student?" he asked. I gave a little laugh.

"Goodness, no. I'm doing maths. But I've always been interested in how we deal with senior citizens." I used my fingers to make speech marks around the phrase. "I was very close to my maternal grandparents and when they…" I broke off and bit my lip.

A group of third years strolled into the library chatting noisily and Justin flicked an irritated glance in their direction.

"Look," he said, "Can I buy you coffee after my shift's over?"

And just like that, it was game on!

Coffee morphed into supper—and our discussion on aging and the elderly soon moved on, much to my relief, to more general topics. We had so much in common; books we'd read, films we'd seen, places we wanted to visit. Our tastes in music didn't coincide—and wouldn't do so unless the London Philharmonic started playing trash metal songs—but you can't have everything. Just before eight, Justin looked at his watch and waved to the waiter for the bill.

"I'm sorry, Andrea, I've got to go. Can I see you again, tomorrow—if your studying can stand another evening out?"

"Oh I think I can manage that," I replied with a grin.

"Great; I'll see you in the library and we'll set up the time and place." Then stooping to kiss me on the cheek, he grabbed his coat and dashed out of the restaurant.

Over the next three weeks, I spent many hours in the library, not necessarily working—and we went out for a meal or a drink every couple of days. Once, I suggested we go to see a film, but when he heard it didn't start until eight thirty at night, he shook his head.

"I can't do late evenings," he said. "How about taking in a matinee on Saturday afternoon?"

He was a perfect gentleman, which was a surprisingly refreshing change. There was none of the fevered groping on the dark paths across the campus that undergraduates mistake for "courting" as my Gran used to call it. My Gran would have approved of Justin. We'd progressed from a chaste kiss on the cheek to something a little more passionate, but he seemed to be taking things very slowly. Then one evening, he took my hand and looked deep into my eyes.

"Andrea, it's your birthday next weekend. I've got an idea how we can celebrate." How on earth did he know? "I work in the library," he said with a grin, seeing my confusion. "It's not difficult to find information about someone if I need to."

"Right," I said, "well, I don't usually celebrate…"

"Andrea," he put up his hand to stop me, "We've had

such a wonderful time these past three weeks, so I want to do something special." He smiled and went on: "I'm going to take you to have tea with my Grandmother Bethany!" It wasn't exactly the most exciting offer I'd ever had—but I was the one who said she didn't do birthdays anyway.

"Gran, we're here, where are you?" The front door was wide open and a deafening silence met Justin's words. He ran through the house, checking every room. Then he came back into the garden and stood with his fingers buried in his hair, looking around wildly.

"Are you looking for me, dear?" an ancient woman said softly from the gate.

"Gran, where have you been? And why was the front door open?" Justin pushed past me in his haste to reach her.

"I went to the post box. I couldn't remember where the keys are, so I left the door open." She leaned heavily on his arm as they walked up the path, straight past me and into the house. I swear if I'd not moved quickly, they would have shut the door in my face.

Justin remembered me once he'd settled Bethany in her chair, and introduced me as his young lady. It felt sort of nice, if a little dated. She glanced at me and went back to complaining about a neighbour's dog barking all night.

I handed over a tin of her favourite Bakewell tarts—and she barely nodded her thanks. It was a good job it was Cissie who'd slaved over them—I'd have been really hacked off if she'd treated my efforts like that.

"I'll put the kettle on and we'll have these with our tea," said Justin. I offered to help, but he shook his head. "You stay here, Andrea. I want you and Gran to become friends." Well, I couldn't see that happening, but I turned to her with a smile.

"What do you do for a living?" she asked, startling me with the harshness of her voice now we were alone.

"I'm a student at the University."

"He hasn't got any money, you know."

"I don't want his money."

"Of course you do! Every woman he brings home is after his money. But he hasn't got any. This house is mine. Everything is mine."

I opened my mouth to argue, but at that moment, Justin returned and the mean-mouthed sharp-eyed woman turned back into a vague, kindly grandmother. Wow, you're good, lady; I'll give you that, I thought. Justin poured the tea and handed Bethany one of Cissie's tarts.

"Andrea made these for you, Gran," he said. She picked it up between two fingers and sniffed at it then took a tiny, ladylike bite.

"They're very dry," she said, "and there's a strange taste in the background. What is it?"

I knew I should have listened when Cissie read out the recipe. She'd mentioned a special ingredient, an old family secret.

"Oh, that's a family secret," I said. "I could tell you, but then I'd have to ki—"

"Gran, tell Andrea about when you used to work in the tea-shop in Bristol," cut in Justin, throwing me a sharp look. I guess threatening to kill your boyfriend's grandmother on the first meeting is rather extreme.

For the next hour, I heard all about Bethany's early life. It was a typical oldie's ramble and I would have dropped off a couple of times, except Justin gave my arm a squeeze every so often. Finally she leaned back in the chair and closed her eyes. Justin stood and whispered to me.

"I'll just pop these tea things in the kitchen and then we'll go. She needs her afternoon nap."

As he walked out of the room, Bethany's eyes flew open and she stared at me. There was none of the doddery old lady in that stare; just pure dislike. There was a lot more going on in that old head than Justin realised. I didn't think I would get too many invitations to take tea with Bethany and I wasn't unhappy at that thought.

On the Monday, I popped into the library on my way to lectures to say good morning to Justin. He looked distracted and said he didn't have time to talk.

"But there's something I need to tell you," he went on. "Can we meet after work this evening?"

We met at five in the student bar. I sipped my drink and looked at him with what I hoped was a loving look in my eyes—and it was right between the eyes that his words smacked me.

"Andrea, it's not going to work! I'm sorry."

"What's not going to work?"

"Us; you and me." I stared at him as he continued. "Gran was crying when I got back on Saturday. She's convinced I'll put her in a home and move you into the house. I spent all evening telling her she's the most important person in my life."

"That just means she and I don't have to meet," I said. "It doesn't change anything else, does it?" But he was shaking his head, even as I spoke.

"I was hoping you two would be friends; she needs a companion, but she's so confused, I don't think the time's right."

I thought back to Bethany's stare on Saturday afternoon. Dislike, certainly; calculation too. But the one thing I hadn't seen in it was confusion. There was no point in even thinking about fighting her. I drained my drink and stood up.

"Okay, Justin, I understand. It's been fun, but it can't go on any longer." I turned and walked away, praying my legs would carry me and my dignity out of the bar.

By the time Cissie got back from Pilates that evening, I was over the shock and starting to see the positives. No more pretence; and maybe a lucky escape. And I'd changed my clothes. Wearing my favourite outfit—camouflage trousers teamed with leather waistcoat and Black Death tee-shirt—I placed a couple of blouses on her bed.

"I won't need those again, thanks."

"Andy, I'm so sorry" she said, giving me a hug. I shrugged and smiled at her.

"Well, it was fun while it lasted, but I knew it was too good to be true." Then we snorted with laughter,

"You sound like the supporting actress in a 1940s weepie," she said. "Come on; let's round up the guys and go for a drink."

"I've been thinking, Cissie," I said as we got ready to go out, "what this room needs to finish it off is some new curtains. I saw the most wonderful black and white gingham in town last week."

She looked at me closely, obviously suspecting sarcasm, then grinned and nodded.

"Okay, you're on—but only if we finish them off with a couple of black leather tie-backs!"

March: The Honeybee Mafia

Melanie's scream ripped through the early morning hubbub at Beehives, just as the residents were settling down to breakfast. Freda Fellowes jumped in her seat, dropped her spoon back into her porridge and exclaimed loudly as the thick liquid flew up.

"Now look what's happened! I've got porridge on my best cardigan," she wailed, scrubbing at the embroidered roses with her napkin. She always wore this cardigan on Wednesdays, since one of the window cleaners told her it matched the blue of her eyes.

All the others stopped what they were doing to see who was causing the commotion. Even Gilbert Hodges sensed there was something amiss, and he wasn't wearing his hearing aid. He never did wear it before noon, saying he enjoyed the peace and tranquillity.

Jennie and Flora came out of the kitchen, expecting to see one of the residents collapsed (or worse!). Jennie was running, with a look of concern on her face, like a mother lion hearing a distressed cub.

"Come on Flora, get a move on. I may need your help," she called, looking over her shoulder. Her auburn hair swung around her face and her many bangles clicked like castanets.

"I'm doing the best I can, Jennie." grumbled Flora, "You know I have to watch my breathing problems—and my feet are really playing me up this week."

Flora would never be a good advertisement for the low-cholesterol spread that shared her name. She always ambled at the same pace, whether she was bringing out the tea trolley, answering the door to "that nice young doctor from the local practice" or coming to tell cook that she "could smell burning from the kitchen and how long did she say to set the timer for?"

Melanie Howells was a longstanding and popular member of the community, recently passing her eighty-fifth birthday. She was a small, neat woman, who never came down to breakfast without her make-up in place and a delicate floral perfume surrounding her. This morning, her usual calm demeanour was gone. She was sitting at her normal table, her lips trembling, her whole body quivering. In her hand, she held a sheet of paper. An unstamped envelope lay next to her plate.

"Why, whatever's the matter, dear?" said Jennie, kneeling beside the frail figure and putting an arm around her trembling shoulders. Melanie opened her mouth a couple of times, but no sound came out. She held out the letter to Jennie. But she was too slow. Flora grabbed it and held it to the light.

"What on earth…," gasped Flora, then she grinned as she began to read the writing on the sheet of cheap, green notepaper. Melanie groaned and buried her face in her hands.

"There was an old lady called Mel
Whose clothes had a terrible smell
She went for a walk…"

"Now, that's quite enough, Flora dear—I'm sure Mrs Howells doesn't want her correspondence shared with the whole room." said a quiet voice from the corner table overlooking the rose bed. It was Edith Barstock, a recent arrival at Beehives.

Everyone spun round to look at Edith. It was not the fact that she'd challenged Flora—everybody did that. It was the fact that she'd spoken at all. In the three months since arriving, Edith had barely opened her mouth—and never once had anybody heard her start a conversation. She was always polite. She would speak if spoken to. But to be honest, that didn't happen very often. She was yet to be accepted as one of the crowd—or the Honeybee Mafia, as Ted the gardener had been known to call them on occasion.

Beehives, the residential home midway between Coombesford and Chudleigh, had been set up in the 1980s. It positioned itself squarely in the middle of the market. Just this side of expensive, so that genteel pensioners, such as retired teachers and civil servants, could afford the fees, but certainly not cheap enough to let in "the wrong sort of person". The trustees (and residents) had a very clear view of the required clientele.

Most of the residents had been there between five and ten years. There was a sense of routine and certainty to their lives. Everyone had their recognised places in the dining room and their favourite chair in the TV lounge. Coffee was at eleven each morning and tea at four in the afternoon. There was no talking for fifteen minutes, just after seven each evening as they caught up with the goings-on in Ambridge. And there was certainly no possibility of watching Love Island: "not at all the sort of thing we want to see at our age, dear," stated Maude Rowley when Flora suggested they put it on one night "just for a laugh". Maude was the grande dame of Beehives or Queen Bee of the Mafia, depending on your point of view. A large woman, both in stature and personality, she was the fount of all knowledge—and arbiter in all disputes. It was Maude who led most conversations. So far, she'd failed to find anything of interest to talk about with Edith—so she hadn't bothered. And where Maude led, others followed.

For the rest of the morning, there was only one topic of conversation—Melanie's letter. Who could have sent it? Who would want to upset such a quiet, kindly soul? And for once, Maude had nothing to say. She was as bemused as the rest of them. The recipient herself had retired to her room and refused to come out, even for elevenses.

Around lunchtime, a strange rumour started to circulate, although no-one knew who started it. Edith Barstock was believed to have once worked for a private detective agency. If that was true, maybe she could offer some advice. Surely some of the methods used by her bosses had rubbed off on her.

After lunch, Maude approached the corner table as Edith sat contemplating the roses.

"Edith, dear, I understand you have some experience of crime scenes." she began. "We're all completely at a loss about this letter of Melanie's—and she's so upset. Is there anything you can do to help?"

Edith smiled.

"Well, I was much more of a Della Street than a Perry Mason, but of course, I'll be delighted to help if I can." And under her gentle guidance, the investigation began. Freda Fellowes collected copies of everyone's handwriting to compare with that on the letter. It didn't tell them very much as the letter had been typed and only the envelope was handwritten, but it made her feel part of the investigation team.

Gilbert Hodges interviewed the lad who collected the post from the box by the gate. He was adamant the letter, distinctive in its green envelope, had not been in the pile he had delivered that morning. They were inclined to believe him. He always had a good look through all the envelopes on the walk up the drive. He'd been known to tell people what their mail was about before they had a chance to open it.

Maude herself took the most difficult task; interviewing Melanie.

"Now Melanie, I know it's distressing for you, but if we are going to solve this little mystery, you really do need to help us. Is there anyone that you can think of who might want to upset you in this way? Anyone you have fallen out with recently—or anyone from your past that might be harbouring a grudge?"

Melanie thought hard for a few moments, shook her head with trembling lips—and then collapsed back onto her bed and refused to listen to any more questions.

Next morning, everyone was down in the dining room early, awaiting the post, either with dread or anticipation. But there were no green envelopes that day, or any other day for that matter. Melanie's poem was a one-off that would never be explained.

Later that week, Jennie was updating the database Beehives kept on all its residents. She smiled as she read two of the entries under "Occupation". Edith Barstock: author and poet; and Melanie Howells: actress. Then glancing out of the window to where the Honeybee Mafia were sitting enjoying the autumn sunshine, she smiled once more to see Edith ensconced in the middle of the group, right next to Maude.

[*Honeybee Mafia* was originally published in *Life is Not a Trifling Affair*.]

Enjoyed this book?

Reviews and recommendations are very important to an author and help contribute to a book's success. If you have enjoyed *Coombesford Calendar volume II* please recommend it to a friend, or better still, buy them a copy for their birthday or Christmas. And please consider posting a review on your preferred review site.

If you enjoyed this collection of short stories, and are a fan of cozy mysteries, then my series of *Coombesford Chronicles* could be just what you are looking for as your next read. Check them out now on my website or by clicking on the QR code.

elizabethducie.co.uk

Acknowledgements

I am once again very grateful for all the support provided by my friends in the thriving community of writers and readers, across the world.

Despite a return to normal, whatever that might be, post-pandemic, I am delighted to remain part of the Women in Publishing community; and want to acknowledge in particular, the friendship and support from the folks in the Pickle Jar: Alexa, Amy, Carol, Eileen, Jess and Michelle.

Finally, my thanks go, as always, to my husband Michael McCormick, my fiercest critic and strongest supporter, who just whispers occasionally: shouldn't you be writing?.

About The Author

Elizabeth Ducie was born and brought up in Birmingham. As a teenager, essays and poetry won her an overseas trip via a newspaper competition. Despite this, she took scientific and business qualifications and spent more than thirty years as a manufacturing consultant, business owner and technical writer before returning to creative writing in 2006. She has written short stories and poetry for competitions—and has had a few wins, several honourable mentions and some short-listing. She is published in several anthologies.

Under the Chudleigh Phoenix Publications imprint, she has published, in addition to her novels, two collections of her own short stories and co-authored another two. She also writes non-fiction, including *The Business of Writing* series for writers running their own small business. Her debut novel, *Gorgito's Ice Rink*, was runner-up in the 2015 Self-Published Book of the Year awards. The first in the Suzanne Jones series, *Counterfeit!*, came third in the 2015 Literature Works First Page Writing Prize.

Elizabeth is editor of the Chudleigh Phoenix Community Magazine, and a member of Chudleigh Writers' Circle and Exeter Writers.

For more information on Elizabeth, visit her website: www.elizabethducie.co.uk; or follow her on Facebook or Twitter. To keep up to date with her writing plans, and for a monthly free short story, subscribe to her email list: elizabeth@elizabethducie.co.uk.

Other Books By Elizabeth Ducie

Coombesford Books
Villainy at the Village Store
Murder at Mountjoy Manor
Coombesford Calendar volume I

The Suzanne Jones series:
Counterfeit!
Deception!
Corruption!

Other fiction:
Gorgito's Ice Rink
Flashing on the Riviera
Parcels in the Rain and Other Writing

Co-written with Sharon Cook:
Life is Not a Trifling Affair
Life is Not a Bed of Roses

Non-fiction:
Sunshine and Sausages

The Business of Writing series:
Part 1: Business Start-Up (ebook only)
Part 2: Finance Matters (ebook only)
Part 3: Improving Effectiveness (ebook only)
Parts 1-3 (print only)
Parts 1-3 Workbook (print only)
Part 4: Independent Publishing

Printed in Great Britain
by Amazon

22522380R00057